Death
a Byline

Death Takes a Byline

a novel

D.S. Lliteras

RAINBOW RIDGE
BOOKS

Cover and interior design by Frame25 Productions
Cover photo © Kunal Mehta c/o Shutterstock.com

Published by:
Rainbow Ridge Books, LLC
Virginia Beach, VA
www.rainbowridgebooks.com

If you are unable to order this book from your local bookseller, you may order directly from the distributor.

Square One Publishers, Inc.
115 Herricks Road
Garden City Park, NY 11040
877-900-BOOK

Library of Congress Control Number: 2019957583

ISBN 978-1-937907-67-9

10 9 8 7 6 5 4 3 2 1

Printed in India through Nutech Print Services - India

Dedicated to Jonathan Friedman

Circa 1986

Book I
The Interview

Book II
Peggy Meachum

Book III
Larry Meachum

Book IV
Susan Kirkpatrick

Book V
Craig Chadwick

Book VI
Tony Wilson

Book I

The Interview

Chapter 1

He walked as if he was being followed; he was afraid to peer over his shoulder. His gait was unsteady because of a morning hangover; his gait was also stiff because the cold wind blowing across the Chesapeake Bay swept over the barren avenue of Ocean View in Norfolk, Virginia.

Tony hugged a cheap bottle of rye that was wrapped in a brown paper bag. He had been to an early morning liquor store that catered to those whose drinking habits prevented them from planning ahead. Needing a bottle instead of a drink placed him at the head of the line of those who could no longer plan ahead.

Tony pressed the bottle against his leather jacket in response to a fierce gust of wind. The fingers in both his hands were stiff and cold and unreliable. He needed a drink.

He approached the parking lot of the Sea View Motel, where he rented a room by the week. The motel was inhabited by misfits, drug addicts, and bums—the dregs of society who neither wanted to help themselves nor wanted to be helped. Their parked cars, which had been driven far beyond their expiration dates, also reflected the inhabitants' economic condition.

When Tony reached a flight of stairs, he heard a vehicle drive into the parking lot. Paranoia accompanied him up the cement stairs to the motel's second-floor landing.

After almost dropping the bottle, he retrieved the door key from his right trouser pocket, fumbled with the key in his trembling right hand, and managed to slip it into the lock. Then he glanced over his shoulder and saw an unfamiliar blue Nissan Sentra searching for a parking spot.

Tony turned the key, pushed open the unlocked door, stepped inside the dark room, and shut the door. He leaned against the wall beside the door and hugged the bottle. Then he eased toward the window's Venetian blind, raised a single aluminum slat, and discovered that the vehicle was gone. He laughed. "Get a hold of yourself."

After releasing the slat, he approached a table that was pushed against another window and pulled the bottle from the paper bag. He tossed the brown bag toward the overfilled trash can and missed.

He placed the bottle on the table, took off his leather jacket, and threw it on the bed. "I need a drink."

Tony grabbed the bottle, twisted open the bottle's cap, and poured himself a drink. He picked up the glass, tossed down the rye, and poured himself another. A tap on the door prevented him from reaching for the glass.

He leaned across the table toward the Venetian blind again and lifted a single slat.

A woman. Pretty. Small. Fair. Delicate features. Short brown hair. Harmless.

He opened the door, and allowed the cold and the light and her presence to invade the closeness of his existence.

She did not smile. "I'm from *The National Register.*"

"Do you drive a blue Nissan Sentra?"

"You're clairvoyant."

"What do you want?"

"I'm a journalist. Are you going to let me in?"

"Why would I do that?"

"Because you have nothing to lose."

"There's *always* something to lose."

She smirked. "Then be a nice guy."

"I've given that up."

"Then be practical."

"What does that mean?"

"I'm cold. Aren't you?"

He hesitated. "You're a reporter."

"Don't you want your story told?"

"What would you know about that?"

"You might find out if you let me in."

Tony was amused. "Alright. Come in."

She entered the dark room. "Does this place have electricity?"

"Very cute." He turned on the overhead light, then shut the door.

She studied the surroundings.

The motel room was dark and oppressive feeling. Thick Venetian blinds blocked out the daylight. Mildew from the threadbare brown carpet permeated the room. The unmade bed needed clean linen. The trash cans needed emptying. The yesterday drapes hanging from the rusty curtain rods contributed to the sorry condition of the motel room. A television was perched on top of a steel frame built high into the right corner of the room.

He scratched the left side of his face. "You're my first guest here."

"I can see that."

Chapter 2

The journalist did not unbutton her coat.

She reached into a large canvas bag that hung from her right shoulder, pulled out a notepad, and studied him.

Trim figure. Average height. Dark brown hair. There was handsome underneath his lack of grooming.

He needed a haircut, a shave, and a bath. He wore dirty clothes and a dirty disposition. The rye that governed his stale breath needed a shot of mouthwash. The black shoelace on his left sneaker was untied.

"I know," said Tony. "I'm not much to look at. I know I'm—"

"Just trying to make a living, Tony." She glanced at her notepad. "Or Larry—Meachum—or whoever you're supposed to be."

He picked up his glass of rye. "Want a shot?"

"Not before breakfast."

"Yeah. Don't mind me. I'm a professional jerk."

"Tell me all about that." She placed her large bag on the table by the window, reached into it, and pulled out a small cassette tape recorder. She placed it on the table and pressed the Record button. "January 18, 1986."

"January 18—? Oh. I see. When it all started." He grinned. "An interesting *take*. Alright. 1986. Yeah. What or where to start."

"Fact or fiction. It doesn't matter."

He placed the empty glass on the table near her bag after tossing down the rye. "I guess I'm no better than the freaks that live in this roach motel."

"Don't say that about yourself if you want to succeed in taking back your life. That is what you want to do, isn't it?"

"I guess."

"It's what you told my editor," she said. "Remember?"

"That feels like a long time ago."

"Not so long. You're still in the stacks."

He grimaced. "Is that where you found me?"

"Yeah."

"In the stacks."

"It's a cold story, I know."

"Not so cold to me," he muttered.

"That's good to know. That's why I'm here."

"Your editor didn't take me seriously."

"How did you know that?"

"I heard it in the tone of his voice."

"You're touchy."

"I didn't expect this."

"Neither did I," she said. "But I need the work."

"How did you find me?"

"That's a professional secret."

He grinned. "Is that your only outfit?"

"What about it?"

"You need a new bag."

She glanced at it. "That's my toolbag."

"I'd hate to see what the soles of your shoes look like."

"You're funny." She turned off the tape recorder and stuffed it back into her brown canvas bag. "I don't need this kind of nonsense."

"Look who's touchy. I thought nothing penetrated the sensibility of a *National Register* staff member."

"I'm a freelancer."

"Then you're no better off than me."

"Screw you. My days are long enough. I don't have to listen to you." She grabbed her bag and approached the door.

"Wait."

"Like hell." She reached for the doorknob.

"Please. My real name is Larry Meachum."

"That's what you claim."

"Did that come from your editor?"

"Yes."

"It's the truth."

She released the doorknob. "I'm Susan Kirkpatrick."

"I'm not Tony Wilson."

"One of you needs help."

"Will you stay?"

"If you'll say what you mean."

"You have integrity."

"That was fast," she said. "And how would you know that?"

"I'm a freelancer, too."

"So what?"

"In our world, integrity is synonymous with failure."

She frowned, then unbuttoned the top button of her coat. A short length of unraveled thread hung beneath the dark-blue collar-button of her coat.

"Weren't you running a scam against the publishing business?"

"It wasn't—"

"Wait." She took the tape recorder out of her bag again and turned it on. "Larry Meachum. January 18, 1986. Go on."

"It was a novel approach to public relations. You know, it was marketing—a way to sell my books."

"Okay." She pulled on the lapel of her coat with her left hand in response. "Paint your story whatever color you want, but give me the straight facts, and tell me what you're afraid of." She placed the cassette tape recorder on the table beside the bottle of rye. "You faked a suicide. Begin there, Mister Integrity."

Larry paced the floor as he reached into his memory. He stopped pacing when he arrived at a starting point that was to become an unexpected drama. He turned to her. "I was a struggling writer trying to get ahead, trying to gain that edge necessary for a writer. But everything went wrong. Now I'm struggling for my life and—"

Chapter 3

"—And I'm trying to fix it. I swear. I'm trying."

"I can't take this anymore, Joe. I can't take this constant hat-in-hand jockeying for space on the bookshelves, for ink in the print media, and for time with the live media. How can I continue writing when the people who are selling books don't read; when the people who are selling books keep trying to second-guess the public about what they want to read? They're jerks." He slammed his fist into the palm of his left hand.

Joe was an overweight forty-eight-year-old man. He remained calm. "Take it easy, Larry."

"Damn it. I can't do that, Joe."

"That's Mister Joe to you. A great—"

"American. I know."

"A great Italian-American."

"Right." Larry was in no mood for humor. He sat on the black leather couch that was parked against the wall opposite the desk.

Joe Gagliano's office at Tidewater Publishing Company was cluttered with in-baskets and out-baskets, file cabinets and bookshelves, stacks of paper that sat on the right side of his desk and a television-looking computer that sat on the left side. Numerous manuscripts were arranged eight-wide and were stacked to a height that varied from ten to fifteen manuscripts upon a narrow mahogany table, which stretched across the length of the wall behind the desk.

Joe laughed. His dark Italian eyes sparkled. He ran the fingers of his left hand through his thick black hair.

Larry smirked. "What's so funny?"

"You're sulking like a school kid."

"I'm tired. I'm broke. I can't do it anymore."

"I believe in your work. That means I'll keep publishing you no matter what."

"And I'll live on what?"

"Peggy's working. You've got money."

Larry shook his head. "Our marriage is—well—she's fed up."

Joe rose from his chair and approached his office window. He gazed at the company's parking lot.

Larry leaned back against the couch, covered his eyes with his left forearm, and exhaled.

"You deserve more than what we can give you, Larry."

"Thanks. But don't sell yourselves short."

"We're a small company, and our sales reps don't take us seriously."

"Like my readers."

"Now you're selling yourself short. Your readers love you."

"All fifty of them."

"If we knew how to reach your market—damn. They're out there." Joe sighed. "You know, I got into this business to publish books. I didn't know I was going to publish literature."

Larry lowered his left arm to his side and sat up in response—he was moved by Joe's compliment. "I thank you for that. Forever and ever."

Joe turned away from the window and shrugged. "I wish I knew what to do. I'd do it. If ads worked, I'd dig up the money."

"I know you can't afford that."

"Not yet. But someday all of my departments are going to be staffed by more than one person

and—everybody will be paid a decent salary, damn it."
He smiled. "I might pay your royalties on time, too."

Larry chuckled. "You crazy bastard."

Joe's mood brightened. "I do have an idea that might work."

"Yeah, yeah."

"I mean it."

"Alright. What?" Larry stood up and waited.

They'd been friends and colleagues for years. Their relationship had grown beyond that of a publisher and author.

"Actually, it's more like a scheme."

"I see."

"No, you don't." Joe tapped the fingertips of his right hand against the fingertips of his left. "In fact, it *is* a scheme. And it could be a dangerous one because . . . because . . . ."

"Don't edit your thoughts, Joe. Say it."

Joe crossed the room and closed the office door. "It starts with your suicide."

Larry was bewildered. He sat on the couch. "Okay."

"Mock suicide, of course."

"I wouldn't have it any other way."

"Follow me on this. It's a little harebrained, I know."

"Sure. He knows."

"Look at me." Joe dramatized his presentation with both hands. "*The New York Times*—Headline: *Fiction Writer Commits Suicide. The Today Show*—Morning News: *Desperate Author Seeks Recognition at All Costs. NBC*—The Evening News: *Brilliant Books Released by an Independent Publisher are Discovered by the Reading Public. Publishers Weekly*—Feature Article: *Bidding War Escalates Over a Past Publication. Random House, Doubleday, Putnam*—all knocking on Tidewater Publishing Company's door. Et cetera, et cetera, et cetera."

"That's crazy."

"Not so crazy. It has happened."

"Not in that way."

"Of course not in that way. It's never the same way."

"Okay, okay, what must I do to make lightning strike?"

"You'll have to become somebody else: Tony Wilson." Joe sat on the couch beside Larry.

"You've already picked out a name for me?"

"I've been thinking about this for a while."

"I'll say you have. And what's this Wilson character supposed to do for a living? How does he eat?"

"That's easy. You can work for me as an assistant PR man. Nobody knows you in Norfolk. And have you noticed? Nobody knows what you look like here at Tidewater Publishing Company anymore. Don't bother trying to recollect. I've had a high employee turnover this year—a real pain in the ass. But one that could work for us now. Notice: I didn't introduce you to anybody today; I ushered you from the parking lot into that unoccupied office as soon as I saw you arrive from your place in DC; I told you not to speak to anyone—right?"

"Right."

"By the way, you didn't speak to anyone, did you?"

"No."

"Good. Then we're in business."

"Are you sure?"

"Listen to me: a new receptionist; had to fire and hire another Publicity man; the Shipping department's different; Accounting had a baby; Managing Editorial left to have another baby and raise children; Copy Editing has moved to Charlottesville with her new husband; Typesetting was offered a better paying job after we had her trained; and Marketing decided he could make more money selling Mercedes-Benz automobiles. All this in less than six months. You think

you have problems? I hate employees. I hate payroll."
Joe shook his head to emphasize his disgust. "Anyway,
you're free and clear here. Nobody knows you."

"And you think I can work in your PR department?"

"You've been self-promoting your books on the
telephone and with the print media all along. That's
Public Relations, man. That's part of what PR is all
about." He shook a finger at Larry. "It's a good thing
you don't like having your picture taken. And, aside
from having an occasional dinner at my house, you
haven't been to the office for . . . for—hey, it's been
months."

"I've been working on a new book and—"

"Fine, fine, good boy—you're a true author.
That's what you're supposed to do; that's worked in
our favor. In fact, as far as I'm concerned, you're a
great author because you don't harass my staff. That's
rare. Very rare. So, now you can hide behind your
anonymity as Douglas's PR assistant."

"Douglas?"

"My latest Public Relations Director. In fact,
my whole PR department—some department. He's
another incompetent buffoon. Nice guy. Don't get
me wrong. I love the guy. But hell, I don't know
what kind of germ infects the employee who works

in that PR office. I need to fumigate that room. All I get from PR is talk and no action. Look—be my assistant PR man, my first action man, my first voice of reason in there." He caught Larry taking him seriously. "What the hell, right?"

"What the hell."

Joe slapped Larry on the back. "Good boy." He stood up. "But, hey—I can't pay you much, right now." He shrugged. "You don't need much, do you?"

"Peggy's working, remember?"

"Peggy won't be able to help you."

"But—"

"You'll be dead."

"Oh. I see. Are you sure—"

"She can't know, Larry. You can't be living with her in DC or be seen with her—nothing."

"Washington, DC, should be far enough—"

"National, Larry. We're going to make your books national bestsellers. Understand?"

"Alright, alright. But she's going to be awfully angry in the end."

"In the end?"

"You know, when we finally tell her about—"

"Oh. That. She'll get over it."

"Sure she will," Larry said facetiously.

"Don't worry about it. Trust me. Stop worrying about your marriage."

"Yeah, yeah."

"Hey." Joe produced an exaggerated smile. "Our beers together will be on me."

"Fine, fine. What the hell."

Joe tapped him on the shoulder. "Good boy."

Larry stood up. "Assuming this scheme of yours works—I know Peggy. She won't be happy about—"

"Stop worrying. Trust me, Larry. The scheme will work. She'll be thrilled about your success. And think of it, she'll be happy about your resurrection. You'll see. I know her, too."

Larry nodded reluctantly. "If you say so."

"I'm saying it."

"Alright. I'm convinced. In fact, my suicide might make her happy."

"Don't say that, man. She loves you."

Larry scoffed. "Yeah, yeah. Mock suicide for you, mock love from her."

"Stop that."

Larry smirked. "I'm stopping."

"So then it's just you—and me."

"What about Lois?"

"Nobody means nobody, Larry. You're dead. Fortunately, it will be easy to keep this from my wife since she never comes to the office anymore—like *your* wife. They never come here anymore. See? Easy."

"Yeah, easy," Larry mused. "I'm going to miss DC."

"You mean, your wife."

"My wife," Larry muttered. "Yeah. My wife."

"Larry."

"What?"

"Nobody can know about this. Nobody. I *mean* it. Just you. Just me."

"Just." Larry nodded.

"*There* you go." Joe offered his hand in partnership.

"I must have rocks in my head." Larry ratified the alliance by shaking Joe's hand.

"Books, my friend. Tony Wilson will be promoting the bestselling books of Larry Meachum: may he rest in peace."

"Amen."

Chapter 4

"I cashed a large check that afternoon," Tony continued, "stuffed a bundle of fifty-dollar bills into my wallet, and drove back to DC where I abandoned my car along the Potomac. I also left a suicide note taped onto the steering wheel. The note said that I had decided to drown myself because I couldn't take literary failure anymore. Of course, they never found my body. Joe, my publisher, had followed me to DC in his car. He brought me back to Norfolk, drove to the Ocean View district, and left me at a fleabag motel like this one on Ocean View Avenue."

Susan had taken off her coat. "How can you disappear when you have to use a credit card and identification?"

"What do you mean?"

"Well, even to check into a place like *this*, wouldn't they require a credit card and a—"

"No. Places like this don't care about anything but cash. Look at this room. What's here to destroy?"

She considered the broken leg of an overturned chair in the corner of the room underneath the television from where she was seated. "I see. And you continue to stay in a place like this—"

"Because these motel clerks don't care why you are living here, as long as you give them a nice cash tip when you check in. They also know that there is a no-good reason why we are here; they know that we need to have a working toilet and television; they know that most of us will not destroy what has already been overused and neglected."

"What about those who *do* destroy?" she probed.

"That's bad news for them. Because these motel clerks in Ocean View have their own communication network. Once they put out the word against a destructive dirt bag, even extra cash under the table will not be an acceptable reparation for the offense."

"Really? But how would they know who was who if they were using a false name?"

"Are you kidding? Their descriptions of an offender are remarkably accurate—second to none, including the police."

"That's amazing," she said.

"That's tough business."

"A kind of black market that seems to work," she stated.

"Yeah. They don't have to tolerate anybody's destructive nonsense."

"Still—cash money talks."

"As long as there is a profit."

"Of course," she said.

"Destruction is rarely profitable," he added. "Also, you have to understand that these clerks, and the owners that they work for, are basically lazy. They want to skim the cream off the top of the fresh milk; they want easy money."

"And you're easy money," she asserted.

"That's right. My front desk clerk doesn't care who I am as long as I don't cause any trouble, and as long as he sees a wad of unfolded greenbacks on his desk every week. It's a damn good thing, too."

"What do you mean by that?"

He shrugged. "More bad luck."

"Meaning?"

"I was robbed when I was staying at the Royal Inn—another roach motel."

"Go on," she said.

"I thought I had my stuff well-hidden—"

"Your credit cards—"

"And my identification—yes. Anyway, I went out to get something to eat and to have a few drinks one night. And when I got back to my room, I discovered that my stuff had been stolen."

"Did you suspect who might have done that to you?"

Tony grinned. "Around this part of town? Of course—everybody."

"I see. Why didn't you keep that stuff in your wallet?"

"Because I'm stupid. And ridiculous."

"And?"

"And—I was trying to immerse myself into this role that I was playing. You know, I wanted this Tony Wilson *cash-and-carry* character to become authentic."

"Ah, you're a Method actor," she teased.

"I'm a technical idiot, you mean. Let's face it. That's what I've become."

She chuckled.

He grinned. "I've done that, too."

"What? Laugh?"

"Yeah. At myself."

"That's a good thing," she said.

"It's a pathetic pastime. Besides, I'm laughed out. Anyway—I also didn't want to take a chance of getting caught with Larry's driver's license at the office."

"How was that going to happen?"

"Hell. I don't know." His dismissive hand gesture conveyed his embarrassment. "That's where Method acting can take you. Into stupid."

"Not so stupid."

"Don't be so understanding." He scratched his left forearm. "It makes me nervous."

"Okay. So—about your stolen credit cards that you couldn't use anyway . . . ."

"Oh. Yeah. That's right. Because I was dead. Everyone thought I was dead. Peggy thought I was dead."

"Peggy—your wife."

"Yeah. She would have caught any strange or unauthorized use of our joint credit cards."

"Maybe not so joint. She probably had your name dropped from them. That's what I would have done."

"Damn. Yeah. That never occurred to me." He shrugged. "Oh, well—dropped or not, those credit cards and my driver's license were my security

27

blanket. You know. My link to myself." He frowned. "Again. Stupid."

"Again. *Not* so stupid."

"Alright, alright. Thank you. Maybe not. But that theft was another major step toward the true loss of my identity."

"But you have survived."

"Yes." He indicated his dismal motel room with the sweep of his arm. "If you call this survival."

"Without your security blanket."

"Say—I think you're actually listening to me."

She cracked a sincere smile.

"You're cute when you do that."

"Go on. You survived."

"Yes." He became serious again. "Tidewater Publishing Company's salary, paid in cash, became my off-the-books lifeline. And the old car that Joe gave me became my in-and-around-town vehicle. I lived without credit cards and identification—I drove without a license. I promptly paid my rent in cash each week, and I always tried to be a careful driver. No safety net."

"I understand. So. What happened?"

He glanced at the bottle of rye and considered pouring himself a drink. "Nothing. At first. I worked at the TPC office as Tony Wilson and promoted my books." He took another look at the bottle and began losing his concentration.

Susan encouraged him to regain his focus. "Tony?—"

Chapter 5

—"Tony? Tony! Are you responsible for this?" Douglas rushed into Tidewater Publishing's kitchenette.

Tony Wilson was about to pour himself a cup of coffee.

It was ten o'clock in the morning—late, even for Douglas whose work habits were not in sync with the office's eight-to-five hours, but who twice made up for the time by staying long past the normal *TPC* working hours.

Although Douglas was short and overweight, he was a distinguished-looking Southern gentleman. He was highly educated but mentally scattered, very creative but equally unorganized, sincerely jovial but conversationally tedious. He was a gray-headed fifty-year-old with a Virginian drawl that reflected breeding.

Tony raised his cup with his left hand and the pot of coffee with his right in a friendly gesture. "Coffee?"

"It's the *New York Times*." Douglas waved a section of the newspaper like a flag, and danced a tight circular jig in the kitchenette.

Tony slipped the pot onto the coffee warmer and placed his empty cup on the counter. "And?"

"And?! It's *The New York Times Book Review*!"

Tony was bored with Douglas. After months of working with him, he had come to the conclusion that Douglas was a nice idiot who could ramble endlessly about nothing and paralyze his listener into a stupor. At first, Tony thought that by interrupting Douglas he could get him to focus on his point, but he learned that interrupting him only succeeded in making Douglas begin the story again. Nothing penetrated Douglas's mental disorientation, nothing altered his organizational disarray. And any pause in verbal chatter was an illusion.

"Spit it out, Douglas, will you? Give me the bottom line."

"Larry Meachum's last book, *The Color of the Sea*—look! It's the cover story, the lead review, the top enchilada! It's going to become a best seller."

"Let me see that." Tony snatched the newspaper from Douglas. He was astonished by the size of the book page spread. "Wow! Look at this cover shot."

Tony skimmed the feature-book review from one line of praise to another until he could not contain himself. "It's a rave, Douglas! Do you know what this might mean?"

"Success! Did you have anything to do with this?"

"Hell, no. I wish."

"Then maybe, I . . . I . . . ." Douglas searched his memory. He wanted to take credit for the review's placement. This meant exoneration, proof that he was doing his job. Perhaps he would get a raise out of this; perhaps he might be able to hold on to a position for a change.

Tony pushed past Douglas and rushed into Joe's office, waving the *Times* like a flag. "Get off the telephone. Look. Look! It's happening." Tony set the newspaper on Joe's desk and stepped back to watch the effect.

Joe was irritated. "Marty. Marty. Can I get back to you? Marty. Something's come up." Joe attempted to pry the telephone from his ear. "Marty. Let me, wait—let—right—I'll call you back." He pulled the phone from his ear and slammed the receiver onto its cradle. "Damn it, that was important."

Tony pointed at the newspaper. "And that isn't?"

Joe's irritation dissolved as soon as he examined the page. "Whoa. How did this happen? Who's responsible for this?"

"I don't know."

Their conspiratorial eyes met.

"Do you realize what this might mean, Tony?"

"It's the beginning."

"It's a break." Joe shared an approving grin with Tony. "Larry Meachum could be famous. But how did—"

"It's publicity," Douglas interjected, as he stepped into the office in order to take the credit he thought he deserved.

"Good work, Douglas."

"Thank you, Joe."

"That's Mister Joe to you."

"Yeah," Tony added. "A great American!"

Douglas laughed. "A great Italian American."

Joe stood up. "Come on, publicity department, let's celebrate. I'll pour the coffee."

Chapter 6

"So? What happened?" Kirkpatrick glanced at the cassette tape recorder to make sure it was still running.

"The telephone rang constantly at Tidewater Publishing. The book distributors, the independent bookstores, the national book-chain buyers, the sales reps—all couldn't meet the demand for *The Color of the Sea*. Rave reviews appeared in newspapers, magazines, journals, newsletters, and book club catalogs. Then there were calls from radio producers and television talk show hosts requesting to have anybody on their shows who knew anything about Larry Meachum. Everybody wanted to know more about him. After a while, *The Color of the Sea* was everywhere—in bookstores and department stores and drugstores and—"

"Where was your wife in all of this?"

He blinked. "She was everywhere, too. She was telling the media how I thought and what I did. She was creating somebody I didn't know."

"That disturbed you."

"You're damn right. She was cashing in."

"You were married to her."

"So what's wrong with me—right, Kirkpatrick?"

"I didn't say that."

"*You.* You reporters are something else."

"Don't turn on me. You're the one who put yourself in a place where I can ask questions with more than one meaning."

His hand gesture conveyed capitulation. "You're right. You're right."

"Go on."

"Well, the company became healthier financially. You have to understand, Tidewater Publishing was at the point of selling the furniture to meet its payroll. There wasn't a printer in the USA or Canada that was willing to extend the company a line of credit to print another book. TPC owed money to everybody—the company was dead in the water, and about to go under. My book's success almost came too late."

"But it didn't."

"That's right."

"And what happened to your wife?"

"Peggy? Happen?" He chuckled. "She experienced a dramatic increase in my royalties."

"And you?"

"Me? What?"

"What did you get out of all that success?"

He was surprised by the question. "Joe advised me to stay undercover until my other books had a chance to break through as well."

"And?"

"I listened." He grew self-conscious. "I know—call me stupid."

"Maybe call you greedy."

"No," he countered indignantly. "I didn't care about the money."

"Greediness can take many forms."

He peered at her. "Greediness." He ran the fingers of his left hand through his hair. "Yeah. I suppose—no. Alright. I confess—yes. I was greedy for fame, for readership. Yes. That's why I listened to Joe. That's why I agreed with him."

"Did you see any money?"

"I saw some."

"Some."

"Yeah. Joe increased my cash take-home from his own pocket—you know, off the books. He could afford to do that because of the company's increased sales and decreased debt." He slapped his chest with his right hand. "Kirkpatrick. My book!" He became excited. "My book was selling! *The Color of the Sea* was on the *New York Times* bestseller list."

"Okay. I got it. So what happened?"

"Remember when I told you I was a careful driver?"

"Go on."

"Well, one late night I wasn't so careful. One terrible night of discovery and anger . . . ."

"Over what?"

"Over betrayal—"

Chapter 7

The landscape on the 1986 calendar was orange. Tony leaned against the desk and rubbed his tired eyes. Becoming famous was exhausting work.

After planting an unlit cigarette in the right corner of his mouth, he stood up, turned off the desk-lamp, then stepped into the dark hallway. A low level hum first greeted him from a refrigerator compressor located in the employees' dining area of Tidewater Publishing Company, then a low-level conversation drew his attention toward Joe's office at the far end of the hall. The sudden increase of its intensity seduced him into approaching the edge of the open door, where he listened to Joe's one-sided telephone conversation.

"The poor bastard's going crazy, honey. He wants to expose the whole public relations scheme now that his books are becoming successful—

"I know we're going to have to get rid of him, Peggy—

"Damn. Killing a man is not an easy thing to do—

"Hell. He's your husband. *You* kill him—

"I know Tony Wilson doesn't exist. I know it would be easy for him to disappear. That's not my problem. You get somebody else to do it—

"You're damn right. And—and I don't want to know how or when or anything. Understand?—

"You're getting your money, aren't you?—

"Honey. Sweetheart. Let's not argue about this anymore. Please. We've come so far. We've come so close—

"I know you're solving my cash flow problems—

"Honey. Honey. Please. You're seeing plenty of money—

"Look. You call me when you know how you're going to go about it. But remember, I don't want to have anything to do with it—

"I don't care—

"Yes. Yes, I love you. But I have to live with myself—

"Okay, I'm squeamish—"

"This has nothing to do with my conscience—

"Okay, okay, so I'm not perfect—

There was a long silence while Joe listened to Peggy on the phone.

"Yes. Yes. Alright—

"Yes. I love you too. Bye. Bye-bye."

Joe dropped the receiver onto the telephone's cradle as if he were holding a hot object. "Damn, that woman." He leaned back in his chair, feeling disgusted.

Tony threw away the unlit cigarette and stepped into the office.

Joe Gagliano was horrified. "Tony!"

"I heard everything."

"What are you *doing* here?" Joe stood up. "I thought everybody was gone."

"Gone? Oh, I was gone alright." He tapped his temple with his right forefinger. "So gone, that I was a fool to have fallen for a set-up like this."

"Set-up? *No.* You've got it all wrong."

"You son of a bitch!" He rushed toward Joe. "You rat. *You* and that heartless witch. Who's idea was it?"

"Please. Listen to what—"

"I ought to kill you!" Tony grabbed Joe by the shirt, but released him after Joe landed a side punch to his right temple.

He countered with a left jab, which cut the corner of Joe's mouth and produced blood. Tony went mad and beat Joe into unconsciousness, then spat on him before he rushed out of the office, out of the building, across the parking lot, and into his car. He started the vehicle, shifted the transmission into drive, and stepped hard on the gas pedal. The car skidded out of the parking lot and into the street.

The disordered blur of passing vehicles and traffic lights became so intense that he did not comprehend the approaching threat of two headlights. He didn't swerve.

The screeching of brakes, the shattering of glass, the crunching of metal; the street and the sidewalk and the night sky appeared over and over and over until there was stillness and silence—then darkness.

Chapter 8

"That was a reckless thing to do," Susan whispered.

Tony's eyes smoldered. "I should have known better, I know. But think about *this*—Peggy knew I was alive the whole time. She had been *in* on the PR scheme from the beginning. For all I know, it was *her* idea." He scowled. "Joe and Peggy and betrayal."

"That's a lousy combination," she said.

"No kidding." His anger peeked out. "She was his lover!" He turned away from her. "I lost my head. In fact, I almost lost my life."

"In the accident."

"Yes. I was too angry to be driving after walking into that telephone conversation between Joe and Peggy, after listening to their lovers' talk. Yeah." He turned to her. "Joe was in his office sitting at his desk. He was . . . ."

"Go on."

"Like I said, I shouldn't have gotten into my car that night. But I wasn't paying attention to what I was doing. Neither was the guy who was driving drunk on the wrong side of the road." He pursed his lips. "The truth is, both of us were driving recklessly. I was drunk with anger and he was drunk on—wham! Lights out. A head-on collision with a car going the wrong way in my lane—so I have been told. After that, intensive care, multiple surgeries, plastic surgeries, amnesia—the works."

He placed the palm of his left hand against his forehead and massaged it.

"Are you alright?"

"Yeah, yeah. I get these strange feelings in my head."

"Because of the accident?"

"Yes. Head trauma. It feels very strange. Sometimes this strangeness affects my memory."

"You're doing fine."

"Sometimes it plays with my identity as well."

She waited for him to recover.

He reached into his shirt pocket for his pack of cigarettes, shook out one, planted it in his mouth, and lit it.

He inhaled memory-searching smoke—

Chapter 9

—He exhaled retrospective smoke.

Tony Wilson's face was wrapped in a white gauze. There were two slits cut into the gauze to accommodate his nose and mouth.

Joe stood at his bedside and chattered nervously. "Don't worry about a thing. My company's medical insurance is taking care of everything. I'm glad I put you on our general group policy. It was an easy thing to do. The extra cost was acceptable." He touched Tony's shoulder to confirm Tony's semi-comatose condition. "My insurance agent didn't care whose names were on the list, as long as I agreed to pay the cost of a premium that did not include medical preconditions." He tapped Tony's shoulder. "At first, it was difficult convincing this hospital that you had insurance with me because you had no identification and no family to vouch for you. But I stood firm and convinced them that you were fully covered by showing them TPC's group policy. Anyway, it's working so far. But if and when it stops working, well—let's worry about it when . . . ." He glanced over his shoulder to be sure that a nurse or a hospital attendant wasn't standing at the room's doorway, then leaned against the bed rail and whispered, "Please believe me. My conversation with Peggy was not what you think you heard. You've got to believe me."

"Who . . . who . . . ." Tony muttered breathlessly.

Joe was startled. "Tony? Can you hear me? Listen," he whispered, "you're going to have to remain Tony Wilson until you're well again. The insurance won't cover you if they find out, well, you know—"

"Who?" Tony murmured.

Joe leaned over the bed rail. "What is it, Tony? What are you trying to say?"

"Tony who . . . who are you?"

"It's me—Joe."

"Joe? Joe who? I can't see."

"You're going to be alright, Tony."

"Who . . . who is Tony?"

The silence of relief about Tony's lost memory was Joe's first response, then, "He's . . . he's nobody." Joe trembled. "Nobody at all." He leaned over the bed rail. "Go back to sleep, my friend. Go back to sleep."

Reprieve.

Chapter 10

"My loss of memory lasted throughout all the months of extensive plastic surgeries, rehab centers, hospital stays, and strange places that Joe arranged for me to stay in. I didn't understand any of it. I was in a blur. I was a mess. Head trauma can do that. It can ruin a person for life." He lit a cigarette, took a deep drag, and exhaled gray composure. "I hope I'm not ruined." He tried to smile. "But through it all, Joe Gagliano stayed at my side. Good old Joe," he muttered sarcastically. "He was my best friend. He was my brother. Yeah." He studied the smoke rising from his cigarette. "The present was the only memory I had. The present had been Joe at my side. Joe." He shook his head. "That evil bastard. I'm sure he hoped my amnesia was permanent. I believe this saved him from committing the ultimate act—murder."

Kirkpatrick remained as quiet as a therapist.

"In the meantime, *my wife*, the beautiful Peggy Meachum, was becoming rich and famous on my books—*my* work. Another publisher offered her an advance of three hundred thousand dollars to write her own book." He poured himself another drink and tossed it down. The rye did not taste good. He placed the glass beside the bottle. "Look at me." He studied his trembling hand as if he didn't understand what he was looking at. "Look at what's happened to me." He closed his eyes as he took a drag from his cigarette, then held the smoke in his lungs for a few moments. He opened his eyes, as thoughtful smoke escaped through his nostrils. "Okay. Okay."

He turned away from her and paced the room as he searched for more memory of himself. "Where was I in this story? Oh—"

Chapter 11

"—Yes." He stopped pacing. "I remember."

When Tony recovered from his amnesia, it was an abrupt event one night that startled him into the present with a multitude of questions and recollections that kept him awake. The reoccurring memory of Joe's telephone conversation with Peggy at the office was emotionally devastating.

He touched his face with his right hand and somehow knew why his face was wrapped with gauze. He explored the four openings in the gauge that accommodated his eyes and nose and mouth.

A funny thing, this amnesia, he thought. He had awakened from a strange darkness and, yet, he was now able to remember elements of both lives—past and present.

Tony pressed the fingers of his left hand against his face. There was no pain and no swelling—but more memory, suddenly, about a man expressing concern over his emotional recovery from trauma.

Wait, Tony thought. *That man was a doctor. Wait. A psychiatrist. Yes.* He was concerned about . . . about what?

A strange face?

The doctor wanted to protect him from the trauma of what?

A disfigured face?

Tony grabbed both bed rails and pulled on them in response to his anxiety. When he released the bed rails he exhaled into the unknown of a long night, which ended when Douglas and the accounts clerk, Rita, visited him early that morning. They were people he had come to know, like Joe, during his amnesia. But now, he also recognized them from his past. He wanted to greet them with a more familiar tone, but he resisted the temptation.

They approached his bedside with hangdog expressions on their faces.

"What's wrong?" Tony asked. He sat up in bed, lowered the right bed rail, and swung his legs over the side.

"I don't know how to say this," said Douglas.

"It's a real tragedy," Rita declared. "It's all so sad. I'm sorry."

"What she's *trying* to say is that Tidewater Publishing's warehouse burned down last night."

"What?" He noted that their sad expressions deepened. "And?"

"It's Joe. He . . . he died in the fire."

"No!" Tony got out of bed. "How did that happen?"

"I brought the newspaper."

Tony snatched it from him. "What does it say?"

"Below the fold," said Douglas. "I figured you'd want to read it."

Tony read the headline. "'*Local Publisher Perishes in Blaze.*' Damn. I've got to get out of here."

"Take it easy." Rita placed a sympathetic hand on Tony's right forearm.

Tony crumpled the newspaper as if he were trying to squeeze out more information from it. "There's nothing in here about how it happened."

"Nobody knows that yet," said Douglas. "The article says that the police and the arson investigators won't reveal any more information until their investigation is complete. Last paragraph."

Tony opened the crumpled paper and scanned the paragraph. "Yeah. Okay. I see that now. But why an investigation?"

"I don't know," said Douglas. "It's a fatality. And I suppose the investigators are being thorough."

"I see." Tony tossed the paper onto the bed. "Does anybody know how Joe died?"

"On the radio this morning," said Rita, "I heard that a tall wooden tier of books collapsed and crushed him. They're sure he died instantly."

Tony leaned against his hospital bed. "Sure. Instantly." He was exhausted.

Douglas glanced furtively at Rita before he addressed Tony again. "Of course, the company is in disarray because, well, Joe was the owner."

"He has a wife," said Tony.

"True."

"His wife is competent enough to take over the company," Tony added.

"If you say so."

"Or sell it."

"I see," Douglas said, with raised eyebrows.

"What a shame. The company was finally out of debt." Tony shook his head. "In fact, Tidewater

Pub has been making money because of Meachum's books. You know that."

"I do. But apparently the company hasn't made enough money to raise our salaries."

"I'm not surprised," said Tony. "You know how tight Joe is."

"Was," Douglas corrected.

Tony stepped away from the bed. "I'm certain that the warehouse was insured."

"Probably."

"The company will survive."

"Perhaps," Douglas agreed.

"Then you still have a job."

"I hope so." Douglas grinned. "It seems you know a lot about the company and—"

"Inside knowledge about the company is not classified Top Secret," Tony scoffed. "You know how Joe liked to talk."

Douglas squinted. "That's true."

"Is there anything we can do for you?" Rita asked.

"No. Thank you, Rita." He hesitated. "Douglas. Rita. I've got to tell you something that's going to sound pretty outrageous."

"Nothing surprises me these days," said Douglas.

Rita nudged Douglas, then frowned at him. "You can tell us anything. No matter what it is, you can count on us, Tony."

"That's just it: Tony Wilson doesn't exist."

Douglas and Rita exchanged alarmed glances. They waited to hear more.

"That's it," he said.

"Was that a joke?" Douglas asked. "Where's the punchline?"

"There's no punchline. I'm Larry Meachum."

Douglas and Rita laughed involuntarily.

"I'm sorry," said Douglas. "Forgive me." He peeked at Rita. "Forgive us. But your automobile accident might have caused more damage to your head than a serious loss of memory."

"There's nothing wrong with my mind, Douglas. My amnesia—it's gone. Believe me, I'm perfectly alright."

"Sure, you are," said Douglas.

"It's the truth. Joe planned the whole thing."

"*What* thing?" Rita asked cautiously.

"The scheme. He made up this character for me and called him 'Tony Wilson'—that's me, promoting Larry Meachum."

Rita approached him and placed a gentle hand on his right shoulder. "But, honey, Larry Meachum is dead."

"We faked my suicide."

"Sure you did."

"It's the truth!"

"Take it easy, honey. Get a nurse, Douglas."

"No. Wait. Don't you remember? They never found the body."

"That's not unusual, dear. Bodies are often lost under those conditions."

"That's not what happened, Rita. Joe followed me to DC in his car and—"

"Get the nurse, Douglas."

"You're not listening to me. I tell you, I'm Larry Meachum."

Douglas hurried out of the hospital room. Rita decided to follow him.

"Wait! Douglas! Rita! I'm Larry Meachum. I'm Larry Meachum!"

Chapter 12

"So. They didn't believe anything you told them." Kirkpatrick poured herself a glass of water from the bathroom sink's faucet, then sat down at the table.

"Not a word. *And* they didn't come back with a nurse."

"That's strange."

"That's what I thought as well. Then I realized, after what happened *instead*, that they hadn't said anything to the hospital staff about my crazy Meachum declaration."

"What happened?"

He poured himself a rye, tossed it down, and grimaced. "I don't know why I drink this stuff." He set the glass on the table and glanced at her. "I'll tell you what happened. A police officer entered my room *instead*."

"*Really*."

"It was coincidental."

"That's an understatement."

"I know, it's hard to believe."

"I believe you."

"The officer was nice and professional as he explained that he knew that I had worked at Tidewater Publishing Company, and that Joe Gagliano's death was under routine investigation. I wanted to reveal my true identity again, but I told him that I couldn't remember working at Tidewater Publishing instead. His sympathetic expression revealed that he had been told about Mr. Tony Wilson's amnesia— that's how he had addressed me."

"I see. And that's when you realized that Douglas and Rita hadn't said anything about your being Meachum."

"Right."

"And the officer?"

"Well, he continued to question me, despite knowing about amnesia. He asked me about the warehouse fire, and about my fellow coworkers. I told him I couldn't remember anything. That's when his patient smile flattened, and his line of questioning changed to my auto accident and to the fatality associated with it. When I realized this was the primary reason for his visit, I was glad I hadn't attempted to reveal my identity again. The officer explained that because of the fatality, he needed to know more about my accident. Again, I told him that I couldn't remember anything. He ignored my answer by asking me where my license was since the 'Tony Wilson' in their system did not appear to be me. Once again, I told him that I couldn't remember. And when he inquired about my registration and about the ownership of my vehicle, I realized that I was a criminal suspect. Couldn't remember, I said with finality. He didn't like the tone of my answer, but he let it go. Larry Meachum was screaming to tell him the truth about himself, but he—that is, I, Tony Wilson, couldn't. When the officer left, I knew I had to get out of that hospital. I knew that the police department would continue to investigate me."

She leaned toward him. "What did you do?"

"Well, that afternoon, the nurse unwrapped the bandages from my face for the last time—doctor's orders. I didn't know why a doctor wasn't there for my final unveiling but, well—the nurse was beautiful, and she was very nice. When she held the mirror to my face, I took it from her and looked at myself. You know, the self that was not me any longer. I mean, this isn't my face."

"It's a handsome face."

"Do you really think so?"

"Honestly. I wouldn't lie about a thing like that."

Tony walked into the bathroom and approached the mirror above the sink. Kirkpatrick followed him.

"That face. I still don't know that face, Kirkpatrick."

"It's Susan. It's a good face. Nothing to be ashamed of."

He examined himself. "Nobody knows that face."

"I know it."

"Yeah. But do you believe it?"

"So far."

"I guess I ought to be grateful for that."

"I meant what I said."

"Okay. I believe you."

"So. You left the hospital."

"Yeah. Stupid, huh?"

"Not so stupid."

"I went to DC and discovered—well . . . ."

"Don't stop now, Tony."

"Wait. I'm thinking—"

Chapter 13

"—I'm thinking. I'm—yes, after midnight:"

Tony Wilson waited for midnight to get dressed. Then he slipped past the nurses' station, down the hallway, into the elevator, and walked out of Norfolk General Hospital. The night air was fresh. He hoped for strength to make the journey across town to Ocean View, and hoped for luck to avoid the police.

Tony walked into Colley Avenue's festive night life. The sidewalk cafes were occupied by those who were drinking and smoking and talking. Three young men entered one of the cafes, bragging about how many beers they were going to drink. A cautious couple waited at a street corner for vehicles to drive by before they crossed the street. Two pretty ladies, who were engaged in conversation, walked past him. Automobile traffic crept along the avenue to avoid hitting jaywalking pedestrians, and to locate parking spots in the heart of the district.

Tony crossed 21st Street and continued on the other side of Colley Avenue where there was no night life. Aggressive traffic drove past him and sped through a cement underpass where cargo trains traveled overhead. On both sides of the underpass, there were pedestrian walkways that ran along its entire length. These walkways were dressed with noticeably neglected pipe guardrails with faded patches of blue and green paint amid patches of exposed pipe metal.

When the 25th Street sign greeted him on the other side of the underpass, he remembered that taking a right turn at 26th Street would lead him to Tidewater Drive—a left turn at Tidewater would take him to Ocean View Avenue.

His growing fatigue disappeared after two police cars sped by with their blue lights on and their sirens off. It appeared as if one were chasing the other.

He maintained a steady gait. His mind raced.

If challenged by a police officer, he would not be able to produce identification or withstand an interrogation concerning . . . concerning what? His destination? His intentions? His—what could he say?

When he reached the corner of Colley Avenue and 26th Street, he stuck out his thumb and prayed.

A pickup truck, with its right blinker flashing and with two guys sitting in the cab, stopped to give him a ride before making a right turn on 26th Street.

"Where are you headed?" the driver asked.

"To Ocean View Avenue."

"You're in luck." The driver's left thumb pointed toward the rear of his pickup. "Hop on."

Tony climbed into the truck and sat on the floor of the empty flatbed with his back against the cab. He placed his right arm along the top of the truck's sidewall as the truck lurched forward and accelerated. He relaxed, despite the frequent jolts of the ride. He felt lucky. He had caught a quick and easy ride. He studied the city from a rearview perspective.

There were lots of intersections with traffic lights: Colonial Avenue, Llewellen Street, Granby Street, Monticello Avenue, Church Street. There were many old, two-story wood-framed structures in need of repair in this forgotten part of the city.

After veering left on a wide curve in the road, they crossed over the Lafayette River on an expansive bridge. The condition of the houses in this area improved and, after another long curve in the road, 26th Street changed into Lafayette Street.

Tony was feeling safer.

They stopped briefly at a red traffic light at the corner of Lafayette Street and Tidewater Drive, turned left, passed an old neighborhood diner, and accelerated along a darker Tidewater Drive. An occasional street lamp invaded the gloom. Intermittent headlights altered preconditioned shadows. Traffic lights assaulted intersections with their changing green and yellow and red colors. A pedestrian was a rare sight.

Again, there were numerous intersections with traffic lights: Alsace Avenue, Cromwell Drive, Norview Avenue. They traveled over a bridge that spanned over an industrial area with railroad tracks, then hastened past more traffic lights and underpasses: Widgeon Road, Thole Street, a double highway underpass, a shopping center, and another underpass.

The wind that blew over the open flatbed of the pickup truck felt good. However, a hard brake by the driver caused a sudden reduction in speed and pulled Tony out of his revery.

He caught sight of a distant vehicle, approaching them from behind and traveling at a speed higher than the limit. The intense illumination emanating from its double headlights appeared menacing. He squinted for more focus at this fast-moving vehicle and discovered that it was a police car—no flashing lights, no siren, just speed.

Tony slapped the cab's rear window with the palm of his right hand and shouted, "Cops!"

The driver nodded and conveyed that he already knew.

Tony pressed his back against the pickup truck's steel bed and spread his arms and legs like a frightened spider holding onto its ground. He felt every bump and veer and lane change as they traveled within the speed limit along Tidewater Drive.

The truck suddenly slowed down then came to a careful stop. Tony guessed it was a red traffic light.

He heard a vehicle come alongside the pickup and guessed it was the police car. The star-filled sky provided no comfort as he waited for something bad to happen. He remained calm within the rough idle of the truck's diesel engine.

The driver released the brake when the traffic light turned green, then eased the pickup into the intersection.

Tony heard the vehicle beside them accelerate and pull away at a higher speed than normal. It *had* to be the police car.

Because he did not receive an *all clear* from the driver, Tony remained on his back for a long and uncomfortable period of time. He glanced at the passing overhead traffic lights and noted the passing sidelights that he managed to see. The pickup made a hard swerve to the right.

The continued bend in time forced him to concentrate on the stars above. Again, they did not provide comfort.

Tony sat up when he heard a slap on the cab's rear window. The vehicle came to a sudden stop and he came to a sudden realization that they had been on Ocean View Avenue for some time. He stood up and leaned toward the driver's side window. "What's up?"

"This is where you get off," said the driver.

"Thanks for the ride."

The driver did not respond.

Tony jumped off the back of the pickup and watched it continue along Ocean View Avenue. He wondered why they decided to leave him at this location since they did not make a turn to get off the avenue. This brief mystery, however, was erased from his mind by the lights and siren of a passing ambulance.

He walked into the hostile night, surrounded by rundown residences on both sides of the road, and was harassed by the loud drag of sporadic traffic. He was exhausted from the journey, but relieved when he saw the Sea View Motel—his destination.

When he reached the Sea View, he crossed the street and approached the side of the motel where there was a vacant lot. He cut through the lot on a diagonal and walked to the north end of the building that faced the sand dunes—this location obstructed the view of the beach and the street.

After reaching a patch of chickweed near a public access to the beach, he knelt by a clump of bushes and dug into the dirt with his hands. It did not take long to uncover a mayonnaise jar that he used to protect the cash from moisture. It was a relief to see it.

He grabbed the jar, unscrewed it, and pulled out the $400.00 roll he managed to save for an emergency. He'd buried this money, after he'd been robbed of his credit cards and past life identification, because there was no safe place to hide anything inside a fleabag motel.

Tony separated two five dollar bills from the roll, then stuffed the remainder of the roll into the left pocket of his jeans. He stood up, slipped the fives into his right pocket, and approached the motel's dark parking lot. He wanted to reach an all-night Steak 'n Eggs diner, where he hoped he could hang out and drink coffee until the bus arrived to take him to the Amtrak station in Newport News.

In Ocean View, however, there was always somebody waiting, always a predator looking for prey, always a lowlife hunting for a squeeze. As he walked across the motel's parking lot, someone called out to him.

"Hey there, man. What are you up to?"

Tony recognized Blanchard, then cursed himself for coming to a halt. "Do I *know* you from somewhere?"

Blanchard approached him. He was a dangerous character who was always on the lookout for a victim that he could panhandle or rob. He was also a speed freak who was constantly looking for a fix. He wore a pair of blue jean overalls without a shirt, and a tattered pair of sneakers. His greasy brown hair hung to his bare shoulders, and his mustache drooped below the corners of his mouth. Nonprofessional tattoos disfigured his arms.

Tony started to walk, but Blanchard stepped in his way.

"That's not nice, man."

"Look, pal," Tony challenged, "I've got places to go, things to do."

"Come on, man, what are you holding?"

"Nothing."

"Yeah, man." Blanchard snickered. "Sure."

"I'm clean," Tony insisted.

"Come on, you can't fool me."

"It's the truth, man."

"I wouldn't know anything about that."

"I don't have anything for you."

"Look, man, you're disappointing me." The tone in Blanchard's voice was threatening. "We can do this all night. Do you really want that?" He smiled demonically. "You and me, baby. Me and you."

Blanchard was strong and dangerous; Tony was weak and vulnerable.

Tony reached into his right pocket and pulled out the five-dollar bills. "I can give you half of what I got." He showed Blanchard the two fives.

"Oh, man, don't bullshit me with fives."

"It's all I've got. Take one, or leave it."

"Man . . . ."

Tony separated one from the other. "That's all I've got." He offered the five to him. "That's all you're going to get."

His feeble bluff worked.

Blanchard snatched the five away from Tony. "I can use a pack of smokes, a beer, and a candy bar."

"Whatever." Tony stomped toward the avenue to discourage Blanchard from following him. He breathed a sigh of relief once Blanchard was out of sight. He was lucky to get away so easily.

He stuck out his thumb, offered a prayer, and was picked up by a carload of sailors heading for a bar to drink beer and pick up women. They dropped him off near the all-night Steak 'n Eggs diner that he was seeking. He was exhausted.

He walked into the diner's safety and sat at the Formica-topped counter instead of occupying a booth.

He ordered a piece of pie and a cup of coffee.

The man behind the counter poured him a cup. "I'm the cook. If you want something hot to eat, let me know." He placed the coffee on the counter.

"Thank you. But I'm not very hungry."

"Okay."

"I'm waiting for the morning Trailways bus."

"Going to Newport News?"

"Yeah."

"No problem, mister."

Tony stared at his black coffee while the cook reached for a dish and a long serrated knife.

Yeah, he thought. To Newport News where he planned to take an Amtrak train to Washington, DC, in order to—what? Yeah. To what *used* to be his home.

Tony reached for his cup, but didn't pick it up.

Strange, he thought. He was homesick for a life that hadn't been good. Homesick for a wife who hadn't been good, who hadn't been there, who— who probably never loved him. And yet, he was still homesick. He had to go to DC. He had to start reconstructing himself into—into *what*?

He realized that he didn't know who this *himself* was.

Cloudy thoughts assaulted him: fake suicide; fake marriage; fake literary life; fake countenance; fake past life in Washington, DC—

The cook placed a nice piece of apple pie perched on a white desert dish on the counter. "Feel free to stay here the rest of the night if you want. I'm glad for the company."

"Thank you."

When a young couple entered the diner, the cook placed yesterday's newspaper on the counter in front of Tony. "Here you go."

"Thanks again."

"Don't mention it." The cook approached the young couple. They sat in a booth.

Tony stared at the paper, the apple pie, and the coffee. Small and fragile comfort.

In a few hours, he would be riding on a bus, then traveling on a train bound for Washington, DC, to find out what happened to his life.

Chapter 14

"You need to go easy on that stuff." Kirkpatrick leaned back against her chair.

Tony admired her trim figure. "This stuff is the only thing that keeps me going." He tossed down the shot of rye that he held in his right hand.

"That stuff will keep you going nowhere."

"I am nowhere."

"I don't like victims."

He placed the empty glass on the table. "Are you a reporter or are you a therapist?"

"I'm an observer."

"Then observe this." He poured himself another drink.

"You need to tie your shoelace."

He looked at his feet. "What?"

"Your left sneaker."

He was amused. He liked her light brown eyes. "I don't know about you."

"You don't know anything about me."

He knelt on the floor and tied his black shoelaces. He noticed that his fingernails were dirty and his hands needed washing. "I don't know anything about *anything*."

"You've had too much ambition."

He stood up and didn't know what to do with his hands. "Excuse me." He went into the bathroom.

"It's happened to the best of us," she added.

"What?" He left the bathroom door open.

"Ambition."

"I know. Too much." He washed his face and combed his hair after he scrubbed his hands.

She listened and waited and wondered if he was going to drink the whiskey he had poured.

He stepped into the room. "Ambition. Is that what happened to you, too?"

"My mistakes are *my* business."

He liked her straight brown hair and her delicate features. He liked the fairness of her skin and her disposition. "Sorry." He approached her at the table and picked up the glass of rye.

"Are you going to drink *all* of that?"

"You still don't know anything about me." He tossed down the rye.

Kirkpatrick was not impressed with his adolescent defiance. "So. You made the bus."

"And the train." He placed the empty glass on the table, and regretted drinking the rye.

"I was able to sleep a couple of hours on the train, despite all the coffee I drank at the diner. It had been a hard night for a guy who was used to sleeping eighteen-hour days in recovery." He noticed the dirt on the cuff of his right sleeve. "Anyway—"

Chapter 15

—"Anyway." He straightened his shirt's collar. "Yeah. The train."

The morning train to Washington, DC, was filled with harsh overhead light. He occupied a pair of seats. Although passengers boarded the train at every stop, paying for his fair to the train's ticket-agent was the only direct human contact he encountered throughout the trip.

He slept. He did not dream.

A strange click in the rails awakened him.

He sat up and blinked and remembered that it was Larry Meachum who was riding home on the Amtrak train. The past was becoming the present.

Upon arrival, Union Station had a disjointed familiarity. He managed to find his way to the right platform where he caught the Metro Rail to Dupont Circle. Once there, he took an elevator to the street level of the station, walked toward a set of the double glass doors, then entered a city that made him feel invisible.

As he walked in the morning light, he kept thinking that somebody was going to recognize him. But each time he passed a storefront window, an indistinct reflection reminded him that he had a new face—neither Meachum nor Wilson understood those reflections.

He felt the terrible loss of time caused by trauma and amnesia and exhaustion.

A polished mirror caught his attention. He approached the antique store's window that displayed a mahogany vanity, and pressed his forehead against the glass to gaze into the mirror.

He didn't know that face: its nose was smaller and his mouth—different; he couldn't remember in what way.

He pulled his forehead away from the window.

What was the same about his appearance?

He peered into the mirror a second time, hoping to jar his memory.

His right ear. The same.

Dark brown hair. Dark brown eyes. Olive skin. The same.

That was all the mirror would reveal. He had to be satisfied with that.

He assessed his clothes.

Long-sleeved, beige shirt with a tight-checkered pattern and a buttoned-down collar. Clean blue jeans. Black sneakers. All acceptable casual attire.

He stepped back from the window and almost bumped into a pedestrian. "Excuse me."

The man acknowledged the courtesy as he swerved away from him: Larry Meachum—wasn't he?

He ran the fingers of his left hand through his hair. He was becoming afraid of the truth. Becoming afraid of Tony Wilson.

He walked toward his old neighborhood just off Dupont Circle. He walked toward Peggy.

He didn't miss their life together. There had been no love left in their marriage, and they both knew it.

Peggy. Dupont Circle. Northwest. Washington, DC.

He stepped into a delicatessen that he had gone into a hundred times. The smell of the place was the same. The coffee and bagel with cream cheese he brought to a small, unoccupied table against the wall tasted great.

He observed the morning activity. Most of the breakfast customers bought take-out. Regular patrons pointed at their usual bagel or roll or knish while they established amounts of cream and sugar with their coffee orders. The deli workers were fast, cordial, and efficient. By the time the patrons took a sip of their coffee, they were presented with their orders and their correct change.

After he finished eating his bagel, he stared at what was left of his coffee: Tony Wilson had eaten the bagel with Larry Meachum's thoughts.

He continued staring at a Larry Meachum coffee, as he tried to remember a Peggy Meachum wife. His wife. His . . . .

Chapter 16

"Hello in there. Are you still with me?" Kirkpatrick stopped the tape recorder, removed the cassette tape, and inserted a blank cassette in its place.

"Where was I?" He sat beside her at the table.

"You were thinking of Peggy." She pressed the Record button.

He placed his hands on his lap and noticed his stained blue jeans. He shifted away from her and almost kicked over the trash can. He noticed the rancid smell of yesterday's chicken bones. "I'm a mess." He stood up.

"Forget about that." She leaned against the table toward him. "You were thinking of Peggy."

"My thoughts ended with Peggy."

"Do you love her?"

"I *did*." Kirkpatrick smelled good.

"What color is her hair?"

"Black."

"Her eyes?"

"Dark brown."

"Her disposition?"

"Cold."

"Her temperament?"

"Mean. Especially when we were alone."

"Was that often?"

"We avoided each other. And when we couldn't, we argued."

"Often?"

"It's all we did during the months preceding my death."

"Argued about what?"

"Money. Everything."

"Sex?"

"That's the one thing we did well together."

"Strange."

"What?"

"Men."

"I'm not flattering myself, Kirkpatrick."

"Susan."

He shifted in his chair. "It was the only thing that kept us together, Sue."

"Susan."

He rose from his chair and picked up the trash can. "Alright." He approached the front door. "Susan." He opened the door, set the trash can outside, and shut the door.

"Go on."

He approached a dresser and opened the top drawer. "We argued about my job—that is, my *lack* of one." He searched inside the drawer. "It's hard being a midlist author." He pushed the drawer closed and scoffed at himself as he opened the drawer below it. "And it's harder being a fiction writer as well." He rummaged through the drawer. "My royalties were below the poverty level. My literary recognition was hard-won." He discovered a clean pair of blue jeans. "Of course, according to Peggy, that was my fault. There had to be *something* missing in my books." He pushed the drawer closed and opened the bottom drawer. "Anyway. The irony is: When you're published, everybody thinks you're rich." He glanced at Susan. "*You* know that."

"True."

He appreciated her response. "Silly nonsense. The fact is—and I don't want *anybody* to know this—I don't give a damn about the money. I know it's a measure of success in our world—I understand that. And I wanted it for that reason only. I wanted it so that the publishing industry would respect me with huge advances, followed by huge print runs and promotions in order for them to earn back those advances. To me, that meant increased readership. *Readership*. Not increased money. But I lost my way playing this game, somehow." His earnestness deepened. "All this about the money is off-the-record."

She pressed the cassette's Off button with a symbolic flourish. "Off the record." Then she pressed the On button.

He believed her gesture. "Only Joe knew, God bless him, I thought at the time. He said he got as much artistic satisfaction from publishing my books as I did writing them. He said that when he went into publishing, he thought he'd be publishing fiction. He never thought that he'd be publishing *literature*." He placed his hands on top of the dresser and stooped over it in humble response. "He *said*." He reached into the lower drawer and found a clean white T-shirt. "He *said*." He sniffed the T-shirt to make sure it was clean then peered at her. "That's all." He stepped into the bathroom, left the door open so he could be heard, but maneuvered out of her sightline. "So you see, I'm as ambitious as anyone.

But I have my *own* ambition—to write. To write. It's . . . it's all about the *work*. The art. The craft. The doing." A long silence followed. "The doing." He presented himself at the doorway. "I wanted to add a little beauty in this world. I wanted to improve the human condition. But I lost sight of myself because I went for Joe's scheme. I didn't question it. I . . . I should have been scared by it, scared by his idea of how to achieve success. I should have known better. Peggy was in on it from the beginning."

"I know. You told me."

He approached the window, feeling better about his appearance. He raised one of the Venetian blind slats to take a peek outside, then released the slat in response to the daylight.

"So," Kirkpatrick prodded, "you weren't making much money."

"We had *more* than enough. Peggy was making big bucks with a marketing firm, which had contracts with the government and several corporations and a few publishers. She specialized in the growing computer side of the company."

"She was an executive."

"Yeah. She knows something about this stuff called software and hardware and systems—you name it. I don't know anything about it. But I know it's up and coming. Computers are the wave of the future. Anyway, I was a nothing—monetarily speaking. To her that was, and is, everything. That's her only measure of success."

"For many people," she said.

"For *most* people, I think."

"Maybe."

"I suppose that makes me a loser."

She turned off the tape recorder. "Don't say that. I've read a couple of your books. You're very good. In fact, *The Color of the Sea* is brilliant."

"*The Color of the Sea.*" He was pleased. "You actually did some research on me?"

"Of course."

"I'll be damned."

"When my editor told me who you said you were supposed to be—"

"Your editor briefed you?"

"Of course," she said. "But I had to hear it from you before I could determine if it was a waste of my time taking on this assignment."

"So, that was *you* on the telephone."

"That's right."

"And you heard *what* from me on the telephone?"

"The edges of the truth."

"I didn't know anybody could do that," he said.

"Everything is false, an illusion, to begin with. So all that anyone can rely on is the *edge* of the truth."

"You believe that?"

"Look around," she said. "We're all being manipulated. But most of us don't know it."

"And those who do?"

"Are fools who *think* they know it," she said.

"Somebody has to know the reality that's called the truth."

"And somebody has to be skeptical about those who are too certain about that reality called the truth."

"And that's you," he said.

"You're damn right. There have been too many torches lit by zealots who have burned those who don't believe in the reality of their absolute and certain truth."

"I see."

"Look. I also can't afford to work on a dead-end assignment. I've got to get paid. I can't afford to care. I'm a freelancer, remember? Still, I like to do my homework. So, I read your books."

"I'm impressed," he said. "I had no idea that *The National Register* had people with integrity on their staff."

"Don't give that sleaze outfit any credit. Remember, this is yellow journalism and, well, they're not really investing very much in this possible story by contracting me. They don't care about the truth, as long as you're a freak."

"There it is."

They lingered in silence for a while.

She turned on the tape recorder. "Is she beautiful?"

"You tell me, Miss Homework."

"Yes. She's beautiful."

"Very," he added.

"That's unusual. A bad marriage usually disfigures beauty."

"You sound like you know something about it."

"My job can be hard on a marriage," she said.

"Then you've been married."

"It lasted a year-and-a-half before our separation led to a divorce."

"That's tough."

"That's history. But you're not."

"Maybe I should have gotten a divorce before—"

"You didn't. Was she ever a nice person?"

"What do you mean?"

"You know—*nice*."

"Peggy was not kind, if that's what you're getting at. She's always had a cruel streak." He sat beside her at the table. "You know, I don't believe she ever loved me."

"Is that an epiphany?"

"Damn. I believe it is." His eyes widened. "That scares me."

"Why?"

"Because how could I have missed that?"

"It can happen to anybody."

"I'm supposed to be intelligent."

"You're being too tough on yourself."

"Look at me."

"You're human."

"Yeah. Yeah." He reached for the pack of cigarettes on the table.

"Did you love her?"

He shook out a cigarette. "I believe I did. Oh, hell, *of course* I did. In fact, I wore my emotions on my sleeves concerning her."

"There's nothing wrong with that."

"Not according to Peggy." He planted the cigarette in the right corner of his mouth. "You know, she looked so powerful in her expensive suits. She always played it close. Nobody ever knew what she was thinking. Hell, even when we argued, it felt as if she was performing, you know, to manipulate me; she always got her way—I'm weak. I'm an easy target. And I'm impressionable. That's one of the reasons why I went along with Joe's scheme—their scheme, as I later found out. But you already know that."

"And now, it has backfired."

"Yeah." He reached for his lighter on the table, lit the cigarette, then placed the lighter on the top of the pack. "And now, I'm weak—and afraid." He took a hard drag from his cigarette.

"Of what?"

"Of myself." He reached for the bottle of rye, but changed his mind and did not pour himself a drink. He exhaled gray cigarette smoke instead. "Her parents were French. They're both dead." He studied the line of smoke rising from the tip of his smoldering cigarette. "Peggy. Her skin is beautiful. Her features are perfect. Her figure and her legs and the thickness of her hair are—" He shook himself free of her and took a bitter drag from his cigarette. "Why do you write for these people?" He exhaled judgmental smoke. "*The National Register*."

"I've got to eat."

"What happened to *your* career?"

"You, of all people, should know how fragile that is," she said. "Were you faithful?"

"Had no time for anything else."

She was amused by his answer.

"It's too much trouble being unfaithful. I didn't have the time. And I don't have the inclination. Besides, it's wrong, isn't it?"

"You mean, morally," she qualified.

"Yes, that. And the fact that it is the height of disrespect. That's important, you know, between two people. I never wanted another person to feel superior to Peggy, especially with a demeaning secret."

"Was she faithful?"

"I don't know. That is, until . . . ." He bowed his head. "I guess I'm a real nut. That should make good copy for your paper."

"Maybe."

He flicked the growing ash of his cigarette into the nearby ashtray on the table. "I have come to realize that I don't know who Peggy is, except . . ."

"Go on."

"Except—I think she's capable of doing anything. And I think I'm afraid of that and whatever else I might learn about her. Does that sound crazy?"

"No."

"Weak?"

"Sensitive."

"Please." He stood up and went to the window to look outside. "Anything but sensitive."

"What happened in DC, Tony? What did you learn about her?"

He turned his back to the window. "I kicked around town until the evening arrived. I needed the darkness of night if I was to have any success at approaching my corner townhouse undetected. When I arrived, I hid in the backyard and waited for her. Every time I heard a car in the street out front, I crept along the side of the townhouse to see if it was her. When she finally arrived, she was neither alone nor in her own car. The headlights of a black BMW forced me to hug the shadows by the side of the house." Tony took a thoughtful drag from his cigarette. "I heard car doors open and close. I heard laughter." Staccato smoke escaped from his mouth as he spoke. "From the edge of the shadow that I was standing in, I saw a man accompany her into the house. They must have been out to dinner."

He took a final drag, approached the ashtray on the table, and crushed out the cigarette. "Dinner. Yeah—"

Chapter 17

—"Yeah. Dinner." He exhaled bitter smoke as he remembered stepping out of the shadow to approach the back of the townhouse. "They must have had dinner."

The light was turned on in the kitchen and it spilled into the backyard patio.

Tony eased toward the edge of the partially open kitchen window and listened.

"I received an interesting call today," said Peggy.

"From whom?"

Tony recognized the man's voice.

"From *The National Register*."

Tony peered through the window and saw a familiar face—it was Craig Chadwick.

"What the hell did they want?" Craig opened a kitchen cabinet door, reached for two glasses, and placed them on the counter. Then he opened another cabinet door, pulled out a bottle of Scotch whiskey, and placed it on the counter. "Well? What about it?" He went to the refrigerator, took out an ice tray from the freezer, and brought it to the counter.

Chadwick was a top executive at TeliCom where Peggy worked. They had become close. *Too close*, Tony thought, after observing their behavior together at the only TeliCom office party he attended.

She approached Craig. "They received a call by somebody who claimed to be Larry."

He twisted the plastic ice tray, cracked loose the cubes, then dropped some of them into the glasses. "So what? So they got a nothing phone call."

"It's an odd one."

Chadwick poured Scotch into their glasses. "Forget it."

"I can't."

"Here. Drink this."

She accepted the glass, then stared at it.

"Stop worrying. Larry's in the hospital."

"Not anymore. I called Norfolk General this afternoon. Larry has disappeared!"

Chadwick was disturbed by her declaration. He picked up his drink. "A mere coincidence."

"Maybe. But I don't like it."

"Relax. We're in control."

"I don't like loose ends. For all we know, he could be outside watching us."

"Let him watch. Let him listen. He's finished, no matter what he does. He might as well kill himself. Did you hear that, Larry? Kill yourself and get it over with!"

"*Craig.*"

"Don't be paranoid. That idiot isn't stalking us." He drank some of his Scotch. "Don't worry. I'll take care of him."

"You better."

Craig reached into his inside jacket pocket for his pack of cigarettes. He shook out several smokes, pulled two from the cluster, and hung them on the right side of his mouth. He lit the cigarettes and gave one to Peggy.

"Go to work." Heavy smoke escaped from his mouth. "Keep attending those interviews and talk shows. Write your book. Keep counting the money." He took a serious drag from his cigarette. "I'll have his head on a platter for a wedding present." Smoke escaped through his nose. "Just remember, we're on top of the world, honey."

She exhaled nervous smoke, then chuckled unsteadily.

Tony trembled.

They drank their drinks, then kissed without passion.

Tony wanted to destroy what he was seeing. But he was too broken and weak. His anger had no weight.

Craig Chadwick was a formidable man. He was tall, dark, and muscular; he was tough, ruthless, and powerful; he was successful, handsome, and disarmingly charming.

When they turned out the kitchen light, they left Tony standing in darkness—hurt and lost and strange. An odd pain pierced his forehead. He needed a cigarette.

Chapter 18

"You do believe me, don't you?"

Kirkpatrick turned off the cassette tape recorder. "Yes."

"What am I going to do?" Tony asked.

"First, we've got to get you out of this place. And second, you've got to stop drinking that stuff."

"Alcohol is the only thing that steadies me these days."

"It's going to wreck what's left of your life. You *do* want it back, don't you?"

"Yes."

"Then show me."

He picked up the bottle. "Okay."

She followed him into the bathroom and watched him pour out what was left of the rye into the sink.

"Okay," she said. "Pack your bags."

"Where are we going?"

"To my place."

"What?"

"You've got to get out of here," she said.

"I know. But are you sure that—"

"Craig is sharpening his ax in order to make a wedding present of you."

"Damn." Tony wiped his lips with the back of his left hand. "You're right."

Susan inserted the tape recorder into her bag. "Get ready. We've got to go." She pulled down one of the Venetian blinds and peered outside, then went into the bathroom and shut the door.

It did not take long for him to pack what he owned into a couple of large shopping bags. He stuffed what cash he had left into his clean blue jeans and slipped on his leather jacket over his white T-shirt.

When she stepped out of the bathroom, he grabbed the handle of each shopping bag and stood before her with a bag hanging from each hand. "I'm ready."

"That was fast."

"I hope you have a washer and dryer."

"I do." She approached her coat, which was draped over a chair near the table, and put it on. "You better zip up your jacket. It's cold outside."

97

He frowned. "The zipper is broken. Like my life."

"I have shaving cream and disposable razors."

He touched his face and assessed the length of his stubble. "That won't fix my life."

"Let's go." She buttoned her coat, then grabbed her canvas bag by the strap, hung it on her shoulder, and opened the front door.

Tony dropped one of the shopping bags and seized her left arm. "You don't know me."

"I know enough. And I need a story."

He released her arm. "It's your party."

"From now on, there's no heavy drinking."

He picked up the shopping bag. "I can live with that."

She stepped outside and buttoned the top of her coat.

He strolled into the daylight. "This feels different."

"Come on. We talk too much."

Book II

Peggy Meachum

Chapter 19

Peggy Meachum stepped out of the bathroom in response to a telephone call that annoyed her. She was putting on her makeup.

She entered the living room and approached the telephone—a new one with a recorder that Craig had bought for her last week to bring her up to date technologically. The cassette tape had not been inserted and programmed into the answering machine, yet. She considered not answering the call because she was anxious to meet Craig at the Torpedo Factory in Old Town, Alexandria, but the persistent ringing aggravated her. "Damn. This could be Craig."

She sat on the sofa and, instead of lifting the receiver off the cradle, she pressed the speakerphone key with her forefinger to see if that feature worked. "Hello?"

"Peggy Meachum?"

"Yes?"

"You don't know me."

"I'm sure of that."

"But we've met."

She was alarmed. "And?"

"We have a lot in common."

"Well, you better get to the point or I'm going to hang up."

"Missis Meachum, please, you know me. It's Douglas. I am Public Relations for TPC."

"Oh. Yes. Tidewater Publishing Company."

"I worked with Tony Wilson—the poor idiot."

She did not respond.

"I know everything, Peggy. I know all about your husband."

She bit her lower lip. "I don't understand." She reached for her pack of cigarettes on the coffee table. "I don't know what you're talking about."

"Then hang up."

She shook out a cigarette from the pack. "Come to the point."

"I also know about Joe—the poor sap. What a setup."

"Joe?" She inserted the cigarette in the right corner of her mouth.

"Don't insult me."

She threw the pack onto the coffee table and picked up a cigarette lighter. "Go on."

"Joe should have been more careful."

She lit the cigarette, then leaned back against the sofa. "I'm waiting."

"I heard several conversations between them."

"*Them?*"

"Don't test my patience," said Douglas. "Joe. Tony—and Larry."

She exhaled tense cigarette smoke. "What do you want?"

"Cold. Very cold—you and Craig."

She took a hard drag from her cigarette, held the smoke, then leaned toward the speakerphone to be sure she caught everything Douglas had to say.

"Yes," Douglas mused. "Suicide. In the Potomac River. Body never found. Nice."

She exhaled bitter smoke through her nostrils. "Go on."

"Larry didn't like having photographs taken of him. Convenient."

"I'm waiting."

"Who could have predicted Larry Meachum's success? Who could have predicted Tony Wilson's head-on collision with a drunk driver. And now . . ."

"Now?"

"Tony's disappearance before you and Tod finally had the nerve to . . . to permanently do something about him. What an inconvenience. Isn't that right, Mrs. Meachum?"

Peggy took a nervous drag from her cigarette. "What do you want?"

"A meeting."

"Impossible."

"I'll be in DC today. Your address is—"

"Not here."

"That's fine. But it will be at nine o'clock tonight."

"Alright." She gave him Craig's address in Old Town, Alexandria.

"I'll be there." Douglas hung up the telephone.

Peggy pressed the speakerphone key to disconnect the call, then crushed out her cigarette in the ashtray by the telephone. She was angry and nervous and worried.

She lit another cigarette and thought about her loser husband, Larry. She exhaled disgusted smoke, as she remembered one of the many arguments they had had in this living room.

Peggy closed her eyes and recalled a past argument with Larry.

Chapter 20

Peggy slammed the book closed to emphasis her disdain. "When are you going to quit writing this literary drivel?"

Larry grimaced. "What I do is important to me."

"Your publisher sold a paltry thousand copies of this"—she threw the book at him—"unimportant novel."

The hardcover binding split when the book landed at Larry's feet.

"Thank you for your support." He picked up his broken novel.

"You don't know the meaning of the word 'support.' I'm the monetary support! If it weren't for me, there wouldn't be any support in this family."

"Monetary. Always monetary."

"That's right."

He glanced at the crumpled pages, then closed the damaged book. "This book took two years of my—"

"Hard work. Yeah, yeah. It's nothing like *my* hard work."

"That's right," he countered facetiously. "You've done it all. Especially after you landed that job with TeliCom. I wish you had never met that damn guy."

"His name is Craig."

"Damn him! I saw what was happening between you two during last year's office party."

"He's been very good to me."

"Yeah. *Very*. And some marketing consultant he has turned out to be. He hasn't done anything to improve sales at Tidewater Publishing."

"Joe doesn't listen."

"At TeliCom prices, I'm sure he can't afford to listen for very long."

"It doesn't work that way." She shot a hateful glance at him. "But how would *you* know? If it weren't for me——"

"I know, I know." The bitterness in his voice deepened with his increased resentment. "Women. You fair-weather workers. As soon as you bear the larger burden of support, you discover the cruelty of power."

"Larger burden? Oh, that's beautiful. Cruelty of power? Put that in your next stupid book."

"You're a piece of work," he countered bitterly.

"All I know is this: I go to work every day and I earn every bit of my money."

"I'm getting there!" He placed his book on the coffee table.

Her cruel laughter enraged Larry.

"A degree in English and a master's in Fine Arts. Pathetic." She walked into the kitchen and approached the coffee pot. "I must have had rocks in my head."

He stepped into the kitchen. "What is that supposed to mean, Miss MBA working with successful men?"

"Nothing!"

"I said, what is that supposed to mean?"

"You figure it out!" She poured herself a cup of coffee.

Larry tried to speak calmly to her, but she ignored him.

"You're not listening to a damn word I'm saying," he said.

She pushed away her coffee cup and leaned against the counter. She was unable to disguise her distaste for him. "I've heard it all before."

"Tidewater Publishing believes in me, Peg."

"So did I. But you're a loser. You're pitiful. You're pushing a string with failed books. We have no life together anymore because of your guilt and your feelings of inferiority."

"You bitch."

She was pleased that she finally reached a tender spot. "I don't want to talk about this anymore."

"I'm sick of you! I'm sick of our life!"

"Wonderful." Her facial expression conveyed boredom.

"Screw you, Peg! I've had it!" He stormed out of the kitchen.

By the time he crossed the living room, she reached the kitchen entrance and watched him slam shut the front door behind him.

She approached the window beside the door, then watched him get into his car and drive away. "'I've had it,' he says. If only that were true."

Chapter 21

Peggy opened her eyes and dismissed her past argument with Larry.

She crushed out her unfinished cigarette, then forced herself to smile because the rest of this Sunday was hers—and Craig's. She stood up and hurried into the bathroom. She needed to finish her makeup before she dressed.

The Torpedo Factory was an old building that had been converted into a sanctuary for painters and sculptors and mixed media manipulators. Their studios served as work places and sales shops.

Peggy arrived early, entered the building, then roamed from one art studio to another for a half an hour. Waiting for Craig was torture. Living with Larry was intolerable.

She needed a cigarette. She needed to leave the building.

As she hurried across the Torpedo Factory's main floor, she reached into her purse for her cigarettes. She placed one in her mouth, then found her cigarette lighter at the bottom of her purse. As soon as she walked through the main exit, she pressed the lighter with her thumb to produce a flame, lit the cigarette, then tossed the silver lighter into her purse. She exhaled her first drag as she reached the sidewalk. It was a beautiful day, but she didn't feel beautiful in it without Craig.

"Where are you?" She took a hard drag, then blew impatient smoke through her severe mouth.

Peggy's striking appearance often demanded a second look, despite her formal bearing. She was never carefree. Her taste in clothing required expensive labels.

She pulled down the front of her blue pantsuit jacket with her left hand. The button-free waist-jacket showed off her slim figure and the ivory-colored blouse underneath. Her blue shoes and purse and brooch unified her appearance.

Peggy took a final drag and dropped the cigarette on the ground. As she crushed it out on the sidewalk with the sole of her right shoe, she caught sight of Craig.

He brought her a smile.

"Craig!"

They embraced.

He was tall and handsome and broad-shouldered. His hair was black and his eyes were dark brown. He wore expensive sportswear: pleated khaki trousers, collared Polo shirt, Navy blue blazer, and leather Dockside shoes. Craig had a long, clean shaven face with a square jaw. He was beautiful and masculine.

Craig tapped the tip of her nose with his right forefinger. "Have you been waiting long?"

"Forever."

"Have you had breakfast?"

"I want lunch."

He offered her his left arm and, after she took hold of it with her right hand, escorted her toward a restaurant that he had in mind. "What's wrong, Peggy?"

"Why do you ask?"

"I see it."

"See *what?*"

"Your facial expression."

"Meaning *what?*"

"You tell me."

She pursed her lips. "I'm tired of playing catch-up with my life."

"Then play mustard."

Her expression soured. "Please. That's something Larry would have said."

"So what?" he countered deliberately.

"I've endured enough of that kind of stupidity from him."

"I see. You're reliving past arguments with him again."

She hesitated. "Yes."

"You need to stop that."

She squeezed his arm to signal self-reproach. "I know. I know."

"You also need a drink."

"I need *you*."

"I need a *drink*."

She punched his arm to convey her affection. "I'm serious."

"You're *always* serious."

"Does that bother you?"

"No," he said. "I'm being serious."

"You're impossible."

"And I love you, with or without a drink."

She released his arm. "We've got to do something about our situation."

"*What* situation?"

She hesitated. "Larry."

"Stop worrying." He escorted her down the street, guided her into an alley, then invited her to step through an arched entrance after he opened its dark-green door.

When they entered the restaurant, they had to wait for the hostess to seat another couple. The red and black interior, along with the heavy drapery covering the windows, produced a feeling of being in a basement establishment.

"How did you *find* this place?" she asked.

"You *like* it?"

She caressed his upper left arm. "Italian retro. Replete with red-and-white-checkered tablecloths. I love it."

He chuckled. "They also have the wicker-encased bottles of Chianti on their tables. You see?"

"Oh, please. They *are* cute. But I need something stronger than bad Chianti, my dear."

"No problem."

The tables were small and square and dressed with white placemats over red checkered tablecloths. Salt and pepper, Parmesan cheese, and red pepper shakers orbited around each unopened wicker Chianti bottle. The utensils were wrapped in red napkins.

A young lady, dressed in a pair of black pants and a white blouse, approached them carrying menus. "Two for lunch?"

He smiled at the pretty hostess, who had long black hair. "Yes."

The hostess led them to a corner table, waited for them to be seated, then gave them the menus. "Would you care to order drinks?"

"We will have two Manhattans," Craig said.

"Very good," she said. "Two Manhattans." She left them alone.

"You read my mind."

He grinned. "You, my dear, have had a bad morning. Tell me."

"Let's have our drinks first."

"Fine."

They waited until their Manhattans were served by the hostess. "Your waitress will be with you shortly."

"There's no rush," said Craig.

The young lady smiled. "Very good. Enjoy."

They drank. He waited for her to relax. The Manhattans were good.

"Order another," she murmured.

"What's on your mind?"

114

"Order another."

"You're overthinking the situation, whatever it is."

"I want a cigarette."

"There's no smoking in here," he said.

"There's beginning to be no smoking *anywhere*." She looked away from him to avoid an argument.

He took advantage of the broken moment and gestured to the hostess to bring them two more drinks.

Peggy finished her Manhattan. "It's about Larry."

"Surprise, surprise." He leaned toward her. "You could have divorced him, but you chose to embroil him in Joe's scheme."

"It was *my* scheme. I needed the money."

"You wanted it. We didn't *need* it."

"Let's not argue."

"Fine. Fine." He finished his Manhattan, then leaned toward her and whispered, "Now we have to kill him."

She grinned. "We?"

He caressed his glass with both hands. "I'm not kidding."

She placed her hands on the table. "I believe you."

"We need to go all the way. Him. The money. All of it."

Peggy loved this ruthlessness. She needed to be afraid of him. She liked the fear. It aroused her. It made her hungry.

The hostess placed two more Manhattans on the table.

"Thank you," he said. "Please tell our waitress to give us a few more minutes with our drinks."

"Of course." She picked up their empty glasses before she left.

He studied his fresh drink. "You're also worried about something else."

"Yes."

"What is it?"

Peggy hesitated. "A new situation."

"Alright. Tell me."

"It's a real problem."

"I'll pencil it in."

"This is not funny, Craig."

"Then stop kidding around and spit it out already."

She massaged her temple with her left hand. "I got a telephone call this morning."

"You got a telephone call."

"It was from that PR man, Douglas."

"What *about* him? He's a buffoon."

"He's not stupid."

"Will you get to it already?" he demanded.

She shared the details of the telephone conversation.

He told her not to worry.

She told him that she had a gun.

He told her that they might need it.

She told him that Douglas agreed to come to his place at nine o'clock.

He told her that having Douglas come to his place was fine.

She told him that they needed a plan.

He told her he'd have one by nine o'clock.

They had another drink. They ate lunch. They went to the Torpedo Factory. They had their day off together as they had planned, which included dinner. Then they went to his place to wait for Douglas.

Chapter 22

They remained in bed after lighting up their cigarettes. They smoked in silence.

The masculine bedroom was crowded with heavy furniture. The doors to the bathroom and the hallway were closed. Light from a streetlamp leaked through a small opening in the window-curtain above the king-size bed's headboard.

They usually enjoyed their naked exhaustion.

"You were somewhere else," Craig muttered.

Peggy rolled toward him. "Was it *that* obvious?"

Craig took a long drag from his cigarette and exhaled disappointed smoke. "Yes."

"You're angry."

"No. I'm not."

She rolled onto her back and took a short drag from her cigarette. Solemn smoke escaped from her mouth as she spoke. "I called *The National Register* today and found out that they had assigned someone to investigate the man who claimed to be Larry."

"Why did you do that?"

"Because of Douglas's call. And because of Larry's disappearance into . . . into a loose end."

"Douglas's call doesn't necessarily have anything to do with Larry's disappearance."

"I know. But I couldn't stop myself from looking into it after I got dressed this morning."

Craig exhaled exasperated smoke. "And?"

"I called her."

"Who?"

"The journalist who had been assigned to investigate the claim."

"They gave you the journalist's phone number?"

"Why not?"

He studied the line of smoke that rose from his smoldering cigarette. "What did you find out?"

"She's a freelancer. A nobody."

"And?"

"I asked her if she interviewed the man who claimed to be my husband. She said 'No.'"

"What's this reporter's name?"

"Susan Kirkpatrick."

"Never heard of her," he said.

"I told you she was a nobody. She dropped the story."

"You don't sound convinced."

"I think I believe her."

"Why?"

"Because she told me that the managing editor of *The National Register* wanted her to drop the story, and that meant she wasn't going to get paid even if she continued."

"Okay. I can understand that."

"That's what I thought."

"Then that settles that," he said.

She placed her left arm over her eyes. "Douglas will be here soon."

"Relax." He glanced at his wristwatch. "There's plenty of time."

She took a drag from her cigarette. "He thinks he's clever."

"Doesn't everybody?"

She touched his thigh. "He makes me angry."

He took a deep drag from his cigarette. "Everybody makes you angry."

She sat up. "What is *that* supposed to mean?"

The telephone rang.

He exhaled aggravated smoke. "Relax, will you?" He leaned toward the side table and picked up the telephone receiver. "Hello?" He sat up. "Pamela." He looked at his wristwatch. "I'm sorry. I forgot about the poetry reading." He glanced at Peggy. He ignored her frown. "I know Jenny was looking forward to seeing me there."

Peggy was exasperated with Craig's ex-wife, Pamela, and with his six-year-old daughter, Jenny. Their frequent demands of him unnerved her. They were weak and needy and spoiled.

Craig maneuvered his legs over the side of the bed and planted his feet on the floor. "Pam. There's nothing I can do about it now. I'll be there next time." He took a short drag from his cigarette and exhaled exasperation. "There's always a next time."

Peggy exhaled impatient smoke. She wasn't used to seeing him flustered.

"I'm not irresponsible. She'll write another poem. Damn it—Pam, I love her, too."

She flicked the ash from her cigarette into her bedside table's ashtray. She ground her teeth.

He inhaled hard smoke. "There it is." He exhaled angry smoke. "It's always about money."

She maneuvered her legs over the side of the bed. She hid her disdain.

"I'll buy her anything she wants, alright? I'll call you tomorrow. I said I'll call you tomorrow." He slammed the telephone receiver onto the cradle. "Bitch."

"Don't let her get under your skin, honey."

"Like Larry does with you?"

She crushed out her cigarette. "I was trying to help."

"I'm sorry, sweetheart." He crushed out his cigarette—residual smoke rose from the ashtray. "That damn Pamela." He turned to her. "She makes me crazy."

"I'm glad to see something does."

He pouted. "I hope that makes you happy."

"Don't start."

"Are you happy now?"

"I'm not going to argue with you over this."

"Fine."

Silence separated them long enough to cool their tempers.

She leaned toward him and kissed his neck. "What are we going to do?"

"About what?"

She was perplexed. "Douglas."

He looked at his watch, then grinned. "There's still time."

"For what?"

"For better sex."

She avoided his advances by getting out of bed. "For heaven's sake."

"What?"

"This is serious."

He tried to be cute. "Sex is always serious."

"He's going to be here in a couple of hours."

"So? We're here. Let him come."

The sound of the doorbell surprised her.

He grinned. "Speaking of the—"

"No!" She dashed into the bathroom. "It can't be." She slipped on her bathrobe as she entered the bedroom. The second ring of the doorbell forced her to go back into the bathroom. "What are we going to do?"

"Stop worrying." He stood up. "How do you know it's him?"

She entered the room with his robe and tossed it to him. "I *know*."

"Douglas can wait." He put on his robe. "Wipe that worried look from your face."

"But—"

"We've got two hours."

"Very funny."

"He's not going anywhere." He approached her. "Relax." He hugged her. "Try to relax."

She followed him into the living room, then watched him approach the front door. "Wait." She adjusted her robe and tightened the belt around her waist. "My hair."

"Forget that." He opened the door.

Douglas wore a proud smirk on his face that Craig wanted to punch. "May I come in?"

Douglas was overweight and overconfident. The front of his gray trousers were crumpled and his tweed sports jacket needed dry cleaning. His disheveled gray hair revealed that he was too old to be employed by a company that had recently climbed out of the financial red and had landed in the financial black because of Larry Meachum's books; a success that had not reached its employees' payroll yet—leaving Douglas in the red. Publicity Director of Tidewater Publishing Company was too grand a title for a position without a staff, a department without a budget, and a company without a reputation. He looked like a door-to-door salesman.

Craig invited him in, then shut the door.

The living room was dark.

Craig went to the nearest side table and turned on a lamp.

Douglas glanced at Peggy. "I see."

"*Don't* see." Craig approached him. "Are you the only one who knows about Tony—and Larry?"

"It's hard keeping secrets in a small company."

"What does *that* mean?"

"Nothing."

"What do you want?"

Douglas studied Peggy. "Half."

Peggy self-consciously squeezed the bathrobe above her breasts.

Craig laughed. Douglas chuckled. Peggy frowned.

Craig reached for a pack of cigarettes on the coffee table. "Half of *what?*"

"Everything."

"Why half?"

"Murder."

"That's a strong word."

"With a strong motive."

Craig shook a cigarette from the pack. "Half."

"Murder is expensive." Douglas glanced at Peggy. "She's an ambitious woman. First it was Larry, then Joe got in the way, and let's not forget your latest problem, Tony, and now . . ."

"*You're* my latest problem," said Craig.

Douglas winked at Peggy.

She tightened the waist belt of her robe. "Be careful, honey."

"Be careful of *what?*" Douglas countered.

"Quit playing around." Craig placed a cigarette in the right corner of his mouth, then tossed the pack onto the coffee table.

Douglas shrugged. "A wooden tier of books killing Joe during a warehouse fire is too dramatic for my taste."

"I said quit playing around."

Peggy stormed out of the living room and disappeared into the bedroom.

"She's high-strung," said Douglas.

"They *all* are." Craig picked up a pack of matches near an ashtray.

Peggy entered the living room brandishing a revolver. "He's not smart."

"Put away that gun."

"We've killed once. We can kill again."

"Shut up!" Craig pulled a match from the matchbook. "You look ridiculous."

She was crestfallen. "But—Craig."

"Admit nothing!" He struck the match. "He's no fool."

Douglas appreciated the compliment. "I'm not alone. Rita knows everything."

"Rita." He lit his cigarette, shook out the match, and tossed it into an astray.

"Rita Feldman," Peggy added. "She's TPC's accounting clerk."

"I know that," Craig countered irritably, then winked at Douglas. "Welcome to the family."

"I like that," said Douglas.

Peggy dropped the revolver to her side, believing that Craig knew what he was doing.

They agreed to another meeting, which included a monetary transaction.

Douglas reassured them that their secret was safe.

Craig peered at him with contempt.

Chapter 23

Time had not erased the effect of Douglas's visit. Craig was lost in thought while sitting at the kitchen table, and Peggy stood at the counter by the refrigerator waiting for the coffee to finish brewing.

They smoked in silence.

Peggy poured coffee into two cups and served them black at the table.

They knew what had to be done about Douglas.

She sat down.

Craig crushed out his cigarette in the ashtray that they shared at the table. "We're going to have to kill him." There was no weight to his words.

She crushed out her cigarette and studied the trace of smoke that rose from the ash. "What about Rita Feldman knowing everything? Did you believe him?"

"He wouldn't have walked out of here if I hadn't."

"I understand."

"You do realize I had to stop you."

"I panicked."

"Your gun was the right idea, but the wrong time."

"I shouldn't have revealed myself."

"I didn't see her in the car when he drove away," he said.

"And?"

"We've got to get a fix on her." He drank his coffee. "We have to do something about them soon."

"Absolutely."

"Can you get a copy of the royalty statements and withdraw five thousand dollars from the bank by tomorrow night?"

"Of course," she said. "I wonder why he wants the royalty statements?"

"Think about it, sweetheart." He grinned. "Why would he trust us? He wants to be sure he's getting his half."

"Oh." She frowned. "I should have caught that."

"Nobody catches everything."

She averted her eyes, then nodded.

"You'll have to give him the money and the statements by yourself. Can you handle that?"

She nodded. "Where will you be?"

"In the back seat of his car with your gun. Do you have latex gloves?"

"Yes."

"Is the gun registered?"

"No."

"Can it be traced to you in any way?"

"No."

He winked. "Good."

"What if she's with him tomorrow?"

"That would be a break. But she won't be. He's probably staying at a motel tonight. And her—well, we'll see. I'll take care of Douglas, you take care of Feldman."

"Done." She rose from the table, went to the coffee maker, and poured herself more coffee. "Douglas is going to complain about the amount of money I give him."

"Of course he will. Convince him that there's more coming. I'll be waiting for him."

"What if his car is locked?"

"I'll be waiting for him anyway—gun in hand."

"Be careful."

"Don't worry. I'll make sure he drives into a bad DC neighborhood. That won't be hard to do. Then it's a clean shot to the back of his head as soon as

I have him maneuver into a parking spot." He slid his empty cup across the table to indicate he wanted more coffee. "I'll abandon the car, walk out of the neighborhood, and get rid of the gun before I reach a Metro station. Then I'll come home to you."

She poured coffee into his cup. "Be sure to steal his wallet."

"I will."

"Don't forget to retrieve the money and the royalty statements."

He frowned. "Of course."

"What are we going to do about Feldman?"

Craig sipped his coffee. "Find her. Kill her. That will be your job."

She slipped the pot onto the warmer and turned to him. "I don't like loose ends."

"Neither do I." He caressed his cup with both hands. "That's the kind of people we are."

She leaned against the counter.

He bowed his head.

Chapter 24

Peggy felt empty after Craig left the house. She resisted another cup of coffee and, instead of going to work, she went home to get the royalty statements. She also changed into clean clothes—slacks, blouse, and jacket—and went to the bank to withdraw five thousand dollars. Then she stopped at a gas station before returning to Craig's place. Once there, she worried.

She thought about Susan Kirkpatrick until she finally recollected something in Susan's voice when they spoke. There was something—wait. Yes. It was the tone of her voice when she uttered Larry's name. Yes. She detected an intimacy. That was it. There was a special connection between them. The tone was there. Yes.

Chapter 25

The day had gone by slowly. The evening wait was worse. Peggy was sipping a Scotch on the rocks when she was startled by the doorbell.

She went to the front door and verified that it was Douglas before opening it.

He was wearing the same clothes.

"You're late," she said.

He stepped into the living room. "Where's Craig?"

"He couldn't be here."

"I don't like that."

"That's your problem."

"Do you have the money?"

She pointed at two envelopes on the coffee table. "The money is in one, the royalty statements are in the other."

He approached the table, picked up one of the envelopes, and looked inside.

"There's five thousand in there," she said.

He was not pleased.

"It's all I could get today."

He picked up the other envelope, then stuffed both of them into the inside pocket of his sports jacket. "When can I expect more?"

"Soon."

He tapped the left side of his jacket. "I'm going to look over these royalty statements."

"Of course."

"Don't play me for a fool."

"Where can you be reached?"

He placed a TPC business card on the coffee table. "My address and telephone number are on the back."

"And Rita?"

"What *about* her?"

"What if I can't reach you?"

"She's staying with me. One of us will always be available."

"Very good," she said.

Douglas had made a mistake.

Chapter 26

Peggy waited by the telephone after Douglas left. Time ached. It was torture.

She was startled by the telephone when it finally rang. She pressed the speakerphone key. "Hello?"

"It's me."

"Craig?"

"It's been done—"

"Where are you?"

"—but not in the way I thought."

"Are you alright?"

"Blood."

"I've been concerned."

"Didn't check his pulse."

"When are you coming home?"

"Had to shoot him twice."

"Are you alright?"

"The blood."

She hesitated. "Yes . . . ."

"Coming home soon."

"I know where Rita is, my darling—"

"My train. It's coming."

"Craig? Craig."

He hung up the telephone.

"Craig!" She stabbed the speakerphone key with her forefinger. "Damn it."

Chapter 27

Craig arrived home late.

"Where have you been?" Peggy demanded.

He turned off the living room lights.

"What's wrong?" She approached him. "Are you alright, honey?"

"I need a drink."

There were two glasses and a bottle on the coffee table. She poured him Scotch. "Did everything go alright?"

He grabbed the glass. "Peachy." He tossed down the drink.

"Then what's wrong?"

He grabbed the bottle and poured himself another drink. "The first shot . . . ."

"What about it?"

He sat on the couch. "Wasn't so clean."

"Why are we in the dark?"

He studied his drink. "It's different when it's close."

"Starting a fire and toppling a tier of books to kill Joe had to be close," she murmured cautiously.

"You don't understand." He drank his Scotch. "The blood."

Peggy poured herself a drink. "I see. It's the blood. Well. It's my turn now."

"For what?"

"I'm going to Virginia Beach. I'm going to—are you listening to me?"

"Douglas was a little man, really." Craig managed a smile.

She sat beside him.

"I made sure there were no prints on the gun before I got rid of it."

"That's my man." She touched the top of his tense right hand. "Douglas lives in an apartment complex off of Independence Boulevard in Virginia Beach." She stood up. "I know where it is." She went into the utility room and returned with a twelve-ounce ball peen hammer.

"Where are you going with that?"

"To Virginia Beach. Rita Feldman is staying with Douglas."

"And what are you *doing* with that?"

"I'm going to kill her with this. I'm going to be too close."

He shook his head. "You can do that?"

"It will appear to be a robbery turned murder." She stuffed the hammer into her purse. "It has to be done."

He scoffed. "Yeah, yeah."

"What's wrong with you?"

"Nothing."

"Did you get his wallet?"

"Of course." He reached into his left jacket pocket, pulled out the wallet, and threw it on the coffee table. "You'll be happy to know that his death will also appear to be a robbery turned murder."

She frowned. "Did you get the royalty statements and the money?"

He threw two envelopes on the table next to the wallet. "There."

"Good." She reached into her purse and took out her car keys.

"Where are you going?"

She hesitated with concern. "I told you." Concern gave way to irritation. "To see Rita."

"Oh. Yeah. Rita."

"Are you going to be alright?"

"I'm fine."

"I'll call you tomorrow."

"Right. Call me."

"Will you be at work?"

"Yes."

She lit a cigarette and stuck it in the right corner of Craig's mouth, where it hung lifelessly. A line of acrid smoke rose from its smoldering tip.

Chapter 28

Peggy reached Hampton Roads before the morning light. She drove off Interstate 64 at the Little Creek Exit in Norfolk and continued along that road until she reached Shore Drive. She made a right turn and drove into Virginia Beach. Traffic was light. She was careful to drive within the changing speed limits.

She was concerned about Craig's mental stability. He was not the man she thought he was. He couldn't be trusted. "*Men.*" They were always a disappointment. She smoked her cigarette to its finish.

After she reached Pembroke Manor Apartments, she parked the car in the rear parking lot, and got out. She walked to the front of the building and found apartment eight. Then she got back into her car and calculated the rear location of Douglas's apartment.

She resisted having another cigarette.

A woman appeared in the parking lot with her chihuahua on a leash. The dog led her to the corner of the apartment building where they turned and disappeared.

A man appeared from nowhere, approached a parked car, and unlocked it. He got in, started the car, and drove away.

A light shown suddenly through Douglas's bathroom window. "Finally." Peggy put on her leather gloves.

Another light came on.

She reached into her purse, pulled out the ball peen hammer, and inserted the handle into the belt around her waist. After stepping out of the car, she concealed the hammer underneath her jacket before approaching the apartment.

When Rita opened the door in a careless response to the knock, she appeared to have spent a sleepless night. Her brown hair needed combing, her clothes needed ironing, and her chinless disposition needed coffee. "Peggy Meachum?" She backed away from her.

Peggy closed the door as she entered the apartment.

"What do you want?" Rita demanded. "I'm expecting Douglas to arrive at any moment."

"That's not true."

Rita was paralyzed with fear.

Peggy reached for the ball peen hammer.

Rita screamed at the sight of it, turned away, and ran into a chair. She tipped over a lamp after Peggy struck the back of her head with the hammer. Rita raised her left arm in an attempt to block a second blow, but she failed. Her expression flattened as she collapsed.

Peggy stood over her and waited for signs of life. Then she knelt on the floor, pulled off a glove, and placed her fingertips on Rita's carotid artery.

No pulse.

She pulled on the glove.

Murder.

She grimaced.

Blood.

She stood up, found Rita's purse, and took the money and the credit cards.

Robbery.

She rummaged through the dresser drawers and the closets in the bedroom and left the drawers and the doors open.

She was calm and in control. She was hungry and ready to go.

Book III

Larry Meachum

Chapter 29

After Larry Meachum punched the face of Tony Wilson reflected in the bathroom mirror, he stepped on the shattered pieces of Tony Wilson on the floor as he shouted, "You're nothing! Nothing! I'm Larry Meachum!"

"What's wrong?" Susan rushed into the bathroom. "Are you alright?"

He squinted at her, then whispered, "That's not me."

"What happened?"

"I . . . I don't know."

She cradled his right fist into her left hand. "Look at what you've done to yourself."

"I broke your mirror."

"The hell with the mirror." She studied his bleeding knuckles.

"It's okay."

She unfurled his fist. "You might need stitches." She guided his hand underneath the bathroom sink's faucet and ran water over his injured knuckles.

"I'm alright."

"Shut up." She searched for embedded glass. "Flex your hand."

He opened and closed his hand. "You see? I'm alright. No stitches."

"What were you trying to prove?"

"That I'm Larry Meachum."

"Bravo." She placed his hand underneath the running water again. "Keep your knuckles in that cold water." She reached into the medicine cabinet and found bottles of hydrogen peroxide and iodine, a roll of white gauze, and a roll of paper tape.

"Tony Wilson kissed you last night. Not Larry Meachum."

"Shut up." She turned off the water, took hold of his hand, and dabbed it dry with a clean paper towel. Then she poured peroxide over the lacerations.

"*Damn.*"

"You big fat baby."

He flinched. "You did that on purpose."

"Hold still." She wiped away the excess peroxide with another paper towel. "Men." She released his hand, then unscrewed the iodine bottle.

"I can't stay here like this forever."

"Give me your hand." She dabbed iodine onto his cuts with a cotton ball.

"I'm . . . I'm Larry—"

"Meachum—I know, I know," she muttered with exasperation. "But we agreed you had to be Tony Wilson until you were strong enough not to be. And you're not strong enough!" She inspected his lacerations again. "I thought you were doing fine." She rolled white gauze around his hand. "Why can't you appreciate being—"

"Somebody else?"

She took a deep breath. "Maybe this is your destiny. Maybe this is who you were meant to be." She snipped off the remaining roll of gauze with a pair of scissors.

"Now you're telling me who I should be."

"If I knew that our kiss last night was going to affect you in this way, I wouldn't have let you."

"I didn't mean to—"

"Look. I'm on your side."

"I know," he whispered apologetically. "I know."

She applied two strips of paper tape over the end of the gauze to secure the bandage. "I *know* who you are. But your name, well—it doesn't matter to me."

"My destiny. My destiny?" He studied his bandaged hand. "I want my life back, Susan."

"I know that—Larry," she muttered sympathetically.

His real name startled him. "Thank you for that." He looked at what was left of the broken mirror above the sink. "And I know I have to be Tony for now."

She hugged him. "Put away this stuff—please." Then she left the bathroom.

"Where are you going?"

"I still haven't had my morning coffee." She appeared at the doorway holding a white paper bag in her left hand. "And neither have you. Look." She shook the bag. "I brought home biscuits."

"Nice."

"I'll make the coffee."

Chapter 30

Larry continued recovering while living in Susan Kirkpatrick's rented, one-bedroom house in Williamsburg, Virginia.

From Monday through Friday, Susan worked at a temp job; at night, she worked on her freelance articles. She dropped the "Larry Meachum" story with *The National Register* and, in fact, dropped journalism altogether.

Larry's life was on hold until his health improved. He needed to grow stronger before confronting his wife and Craig. He lifted weights in the garage and ran a couple of miles around the neighborhood each day. He cleaned house, washed clothes, and cooked. Life was good with Susan: his anger was restrained; his mind clearer; his drinking moderate.

Chapter 31

Susan Kirkpatrick was strong and beautiful, rational and independent. She had delicate facial features and short brown hair; she wore pierced earrings and rose-colored lipstick.

Larry had fallen in love with her.

Last week she told him that men were all talk about wanting a strong woman; they usually found equality confusing and threatening. Then she told him that he was different.

He hoped she was in love with him.

What they would become together depended on what was to become of him.

Chapter 32

Larry liked running in the morning, especially during clear and beautiful days. This pleasure was interrupted, however, when he noticed the third pass of a slow-moving black BMW.

After its fourth appearance, the vehicle accelerated and swerved toward him. He feinted to the right, then dashed to the left to prevent it from hitting him. The BMW braked hard as it passed him, screeched into a doughnut-turn, then accelerated toward him again. It jumped the curb when Larry stepped onto the sidewalk and hit a garbage can as Larry ran toward a house. He recognized the driver as the vehicle sped way. It was Craig. "You bastard!"

He caught his breath, then hurried home.

Susan appeared at the kitchen doorway as soon as he entered the house. "Did you see her?"

"See who?"

"Peggy." She stepped into the living room.

"Where is she?"

"She just left. I'm surprised you didn't run into her."

He peered outside. "What did she want?"

"She told me that The National Register had called her sometime ago. They told her about my story concerning you. When she didn't hear from them again, she became curious and called them. She discovered that they had killed the story."

"And?"

"She questioned me."

"About what?"

"About you. About the story."

"And?"

"I told her I didn't know anything." Susan approached him. "What's wrong?"

"Her boyfriend, Craig, tried to kill me."

She whispered, "What happened?"

"He tried to run over me with his BMW."

She placed her right hand over her mouth in response to her terror. "While she stood right there." She placed her left hand over her right. "How did he know it was you?"

"I don't know," he answered in dismay. "Are you alright?"

She shook her head. "Are *you?*"

"No."

She pulled her hands away from her mouth. "I should have told you this, but . . ."

"What?"

"Peggy called me a while ago."

"What the hell?" he muttered.

"I'm sorry."

"Why didn't you tell me?"

"Because you were going through such a bad time."

He nodded. "I see."

"I told her that I couldn't find this man who claimed to be her husband. I told her that my editor thought the story was a dead end."

"And you thought she believed you?"

"She seemed to."

"You don't know Peggy. She never gives up. She hates loose ends. She probably figured that since you were the only person she knew who had any possible connection with me, then . . ."

"Here we are."

"Yeah." He pressed his back against the wall. "What else haven't you told me?"

"Nothing. I swear."

Chapter 33

Larry woke up coughing and sat up on the living room couch. He smelled smoke and saw fire.

He rushed into the bedroom, found Susan, and shook her. "Wake up!" She gasped for breath, sat up, and coughed.

He hurried to the bedroom door, slammed it shut, then went to the window on the other side of the bed and pushed aside the curtains. "Get up!"

Susan got out of bed.

He found the metal latches with his fingertips, unlocked the window, and raised it. "Get over here!"

As soon as she stumbled into his arms, he maneuvered her through the window—she fell hard on the ground.

He straddled the window sill, jumped out, and fell just as hard.

They coughed and spat and reached for fresh air.

"Are you alright?"

She sat up and leaned against the wall. "Yes." Her nostrils were soot-stained.

He heard sirens. "Help will be here soon."

She wheezed.

"I'll find a paramedic."

She stood up. "Don't leave me."

A firefighter approached them. "Are you two alright?"

"She needs oxygen."

"You got it. Is there anybody inside the house?"

"No."

"Are you sure?"

"Yes."

"You two need to get away from the house." The firefighter assisted Susan to the far end of the backyard—Larry followed them.

A paramedic suddenly appeared, carrying a medical bag and a small oxygen bottle.

"Steve! Over here!" the firefighter shouted.

The paramedic approached them. "What have we got, Pete?"

"They both need oxygen."

"Right."

"I'm fine," said Larry.

The firefighter ignored him. "The paramedic will take care of you."

"I've got it, Pete."

The firefighter nodded, then addressed Larry. "Take the treatment that Steve gives you." He left without acknowledging Larry's "Thank you."

After starting the oxygen flow to a re-breather mask, the paramedic secured the mask over Susan's mouth and nose. "Breathe normally."

She breathed.

Eventually, they had him on a re-breather mask as well.

The night went long. The firefighters were thorough about ventilating and overhauling the structure before allowing Larry and Susan to enter the house to get dressed and retrieve what could be salvaged: clothes and valuables—all, loaded into the trunk and into the back seat of her car.

The fire department captain had not determined the cause of the fire before he questioned them for his report.

Susan gave him the name, address, and telephone number of her landlord; Larry gave him a nod, and kept what he believed to be the cause of the fire to himself.

Chapter 34

They checked into a motel and took long showers. They dressed in clothes that did not smell like smoke, and drank a beer from the six-pack they bought at a convenience store.

Susan opened her second beer. "I've got family living in Baltimore. We can—"

"No." He opened his second beer. "We're not going to run away."

"But—"

"No." He placed his opened beer on the bedside table. "We're going after them." He sat on the bed beside her. "We're going to DC instead."

"They're dangerous people."

"I know." He lit a cigarette.

"You're not strong enough."

"Yes, I am."

"We should have said something to that fire captain—and to the police."

"And tell them *what?*" He took a hard drag from his cigarette.

"It would have been safer to tell them that—"

"I'm dangerous." He exhaled heavy gray smoke. "I'm dangerous people, too."

She believed his smoldering eyes.

Chapter 35

On the following day, she drove them to the bank and withdrew cash.

"You don't need to do this, Susan."

"And what kind of a fair-weather woman would that make me if I didn't do this for you? Do you love me?"

"That's not the point."

"Answer the question."

"Yes."

"Then it's settled. I love you, too."

"But—"

"It's all or nothing with me, honey. Besides, there's nothing to go back to, remember?"

"I know. Okay. I'll drive."

Chapter 36

They were north of Richmond on Interstate 95 before Susan asked him why they were going to DC.

"The less you know, the better."

His answer annoyed her. "I was an investigative reporter once, remember?"

"And?"

"You're handling this in the wrong way."

"What do you mean?"

"Sometimes, the best attack is an indirect one."

"Okay," he said.

"Do you want to find out the truth?"

"Of course. I also want justice."

"Your tone suggests revenge."

"Whatever."

"Do you really think you're going to find justice in DC with the plan you've got?"

"I haven't got one yet."

"Oh, that's wonderful." She crossed her arms over her chest to contain her anger. "What are we doing?"

"Going the wrong way." He lifted his foot off the accelerator and let the car slow down for the next exit. He grinned sheepishly. "Okay. What *is* the right direction? Do you know?"

"Hampton Roads: Norfolk—maybe Virginia Beach."

He tapped the steering wheel with his right hand. "Norfolk. You think?"

"Why not?" She leaned toward him. "It's where your real troubles began."

He veered right onto the exit ramp and drove off the Interstate. "Tidewater Publishing."

"That's right. It's where the scheme turned bad, despite Larry Meachum's success."

"Yeah. The TPC fire and Joe's death. My auto accident and head trauma. My wife's infidelity and Craig's involvement—"

"Those greedy bastards," she interjected.

He pulled into a parking lot of a convenience store and stopped. "They want to kill me."

"That's true. And don't you want to know who else might be involved?"

"It's Peggy and Craig, damn it."

163

"Don't be so sure. There could be others."

"I'm not *that* important."

"Maybe not. But now, your books are worth a lot of money."

"My books." He sighed. "My stupid books."

"Don't say that."

He shook his head.

"Don't go there."

He frowned. "You're right. Do you want a soda?"

"Let's keep driving."

He backed out of the parking space and drove out of the parking lot. "You know, with you, there have been times when I have almost forgotten myself."

"There have been times when I hoped you had. I'm sorry."

"Don't be, Susan." He found the on-ramp to the Interstate. "You've been nothing but good to me. But I've got to be fair to you."

She leaned toward him. "I'm afraid. These are bad people we are going to confront. Your revenge, the money, your identity, the truth—I confess, I don't care about these things anymore."

He merged onto the Interstate.

She touched his right shoulder. "Let's go away. We can start new. You're still a writer. You can—"

"No. I'm afraid of Tony Wilson."

"I don't understand."

"I've come to believe in Tony Wilson too much while living with you."

She took her hand off his shoulder. "I don't care."

"I know. And that bothers me. I'm Larry, but you see me as Tony."

"I can't help that."

"You're also right. For now, I need to see myself through your eyes if I'm—if *we're* to survive. But it's damn tough to do."

"I'm happy with Tony Wilson."

"I love you. But Larry Meachum is the truth."

"I know. It's a contradiction that I, and you, must live with, for now."

He placed a cigarette in the corner of his mouth. "There will be danger ahead."

She leaned against the passenger-side door.

He lit his cigarette and smoked.

They proceeded along Interstate 95 going South toward Richmond where they would pick up Interstate 64 going to Norfolk—their new destination and, possibly, toward the truth that would support Larry Meachum's resurrection.

Book IV

Susan Kirkpatrick

Chapter 37

Silence accompanied the passage of time as they traveled on the Interstate Highway.

Susan shifted in her seat, then yawned. "Are you hungry?"

"No." Tony exhaled the last of another cigarette and crushed it out in the ashtray.

"That highway sign said Chesapeake." She stretched her back.

"That's where we're going."

"And?"

"We need to see Lois—Joe's wife. She lives in Chesapeake."

"That's not a bad idea."

"She has to know something." He sighed. "I should have thought of her sooner."

"A lot has happened to you."

"That's no excuse."

"Head trauma? Disfigurement? Amnesia? Are you kidding?"

He threw an appreciative smile at her as he veered right onto an exit ramp.

"And that crazy scheme," she added. "Why did you agree to suicide? You had everything, really."

"Everything except love and happiness and literary recognition."

She shrugged. "You can't have *everything*."

He chuckled. "Very funny." He made a left turn. "I got caught up in the marketing game."

"Meaning what?"

"Meaning, I was an author with an independent publishing house that had to compete against a New York publishing cartel. I also had to fight for recognition with a corrupt and overburdened media, and had to jockey for shelf space with financially struggling bookstores. All of the above were also drowning in a sea of authors who were seeking fame and fortune."

"That's a lot."

"But not all." He made a right turn into a middle class subdivision. "There was my pride."

"I see."

"And that's egotistical nonsense."

"Isn't that true about everything a person does?"

He glanced at her. "I like you, Kirkpatrick."

"I like you, too."

He turned into a driveway of a red brick, ranch-style house and stopped behind a parked vehicle. "That's her car." The gutters needed cleaning, the yard needed mowing, the shrubbery needed pruning. "She should be home."

"What are you expecting to find out?"

"I don't know." He opened the car door and stepped out. "Come on."

Together, they approached the house.

Lois Gagliano opened the front door before they reached it. "Yes? May I help you?"

Lois wore a pastel-green dress, which hung loosely over her thin, bird-like figure; short, straight red hair framed her face. She dabbed her pointed nose with a Kleenex.

"Hello, Lois."

Lois recognized his voice. "Do I know you?"

He hesitated. "Yes."

"This is going to be difficult to explain," Susan interjected.

"And who are you?" Lois asked.

"A friend of Larry Meachum."

"*Larry*? He's dead." Her expression hardened. "Are you people from the press?"

"No, we're not." He stepped toward her. "I'm Larry Meachum."

"What?" She grabbed the edge of the door. "I'm going to call the police if you don't leave."

"He's telling you the truth," said Susan. "We're here to help you find out what happened to Joe."

"Go away!"

"Joe's death wasn't an accident."

"I'm calling the police." She slammed the door shut.

"We need to get out of here," Susan recommended.

"She's not calling the police."

"How do you know?"

"Because she's peering at us from behind a window-curtain. Don't look."

"Okay," she whispered. "So—what now?"

"So—I have another idea. Let's go to Norfolk and talk to an arson investigator about the warehouse fire at Tidewater Publishing."

"Is she still peering at us?"

"No."

"Then we better go."

Chapter 38

After finding Norfolk Fire Department's Headquarter Station on City Hall Avenue, Tony drove to the rear of the building, found a parking spot, and stepped out of the car. "Come on, Susan."

The large garage doors at the rear and the front of the station were open. Inside, there was a ladder truck, a chief's car, and an ambulance parked on the apparatus floor. Outside, there was a rescue truck parked in the front apron of the station and an engine parked in the rear apron.

They approached a pair of firefighters who were washing the engine. They wore dark-blue uniforms.

"Excuse me," said Susan. "Are the arson investigators located in this station?"

"No, ma'am," said the firefighter, as he dipped a brush with a long handle into a bucket of soapy water. "The Norfolk Fire Department's Arson

Investigators Offices are on the fourth floor of the Tazwell Building on Brooke Avenue."

"Is that off of Granby Street?" Tony asked.

"That's right," said the firefighter. "It's near the Union Mission."

"We need to see a fire report," Susan interjected.

"Ask for Arnie Smith when you get there."

She smiled. "And who is he?"

"The arson investigator on duty today." He smiled back at Susan. "Arnie is your man."

"Thank you."

"You're welcome, ma'am." He pulled the brush out of the bucket and scrubbed dirt off the side of the engine.

Tony and Susan maneuvered around the ladder truck, went back to their car, and drove to the Tazwell Building. They were lucky to find a metered parking spot on Brooke Avenue.

They entered the building, found the elevator door open, and pressed the fourth floor button. When the elevator door opened after reaching the floor, he patted Susan on the back. "Relax."

"*You* relax."

They stepped out of the elevator onto the main floor, peered to their right, and discovered a red sign on a door that displayed: *Norfolk FD.* They approached the door and pressed a red buzzer on the adjacent wall, which allowed them to enter a small waiting room with a glass window on the opposite side from where they stood. As they approached the window, a receptionist sitting behind her desk slid open the glass.

"Hello," said Susan.

The lady smiled. "May I help you?"

"We're looking for Arson Investigator Arnie Smith."

"You're in luck. He's in his office. Go through that door, take a left, go down the short hallway, then take another left. It's the second office on the right."

Susan nodded. "Thank you."

They approached the other door, waited for the receptionist to press the lock-release button, then pulled open the door and followed her instructions that led them to the second office on the right.

The man sitting behind a desk stopped reading after noting their presence. "Hello. May I help you?"

Susan stepped into the office. "Are you Arnie Smith?"

He wore a dress uniform. "Yes. I'm Investigator Smith."

Tony joined her. "I used to work at Tidewater Publishing Company."

"Tidewater Publishing—ah, yes. I remember that fire. There was a fatality."

"That fatality is why we're here," said Susan. "We'd like to know the circumstances."

"Have a seat."

She sat down.

The investigator glanced at Tony. "You used to work there?"

"Yes."

"And you're here because . . . ?"

"Joe Gagliano was a close friend. I'd like to know more about what happened."

The investigator stood up, went to a file cabinet, pulled open a drawer, and searched through the folders. "Here we go." He pulled out the folder and shut the drawer.

"Thank you for doing this," Susan said demurely.

"There's nothing 'top secret' here." He brought the folder to his desk, sat down, and opened it. "Let me see. Yeah. This was Parkman's case." He leafed through several pages. "Investigator Parkman concluded that your friend's death was an accident. He was killed after a tall wooden tier of books collapsed and crushed him." He closed the folder and placed his left hand upon it. "The initial cause of the fire could not be determined. Possibly a cigarette. *In other words*, this is a fire of unknown origin."

She nodded. "Doesn't it take a while for wood to fail and collapse?"

"Structure failures occur all the time and—wait a minute." Investigator Smith leaned toward her. "You're right. It does seem strange that he would have been inside a fully-involved warehouse."

"Yet, Investigator Parkman concluded that it was an accident," Tony interjected.

"That's odd." Investigator Smith opened the folder and leafed through it again.

Tony threw a worried glance at Susan.

She rose from her chair. "We don't want to trouble you any further."

"That's right," said Tony. "We've taken enough of your time."

"It's been no trouble at all." The investigator continued studying the file with growing interest.

Tony escorted Susan out of the office, along both hallways, and through the security door leading into the small waiting room. Then they waved at the receptionist behind the window as they passed through the second security door that led to the elevator on the main floor.

He pressed the elevator button before he whispered, "We didn't do anything here except arouse suspicion, Miss Investigative Reporter." The elevator door opened.

"It was your idea, smarty pants." They stepped into the elevator. "We need to get out of here before he decides to take action."

"Like what?"

The elevator door closed.

"Like call the police," she said.

"He's not going to do that."

When the elevator door opened on the ground floor, they hustled out of the building, onto the street, and into her blue Nissan Sentra.

He started the car. "Where to, my liege?"

"I'm hungry."

"There's a deli close by on Granby Street."

"That's the street behind us. Will that be far enough from here?"

"They're not going to search for us. Not yet. Not now."

"Okay. If you say so."

He drove around the block and parked at a metered spot on Granby Street. "That's the deli over there."

"Let's eat," she said.

And they ate: pastrami sandwiches and potato salad, then they lingered over a shared piece of cheesecake.

"I'm not sure what to do next," he said.

"Let's check into a motel."

He slid the dessert plate toward her. "Finish it."

As they were leaving the deli, Susan noticed an abandoned newspaper at an unoccupied table. On an impulse, she picked up the paper. The local section was on top and it was folded to an article entitled, "Crime in Hampton Roads." The feature explored the rise in violent crimes since the beginning of the year. While reading the article, she discovered a reference to the murder of Rita Feldman. "Tony. You've got to read this."

Chapter 39

Susan stared at the newspaper and Tony stared at the
Nissan's dashboard as he smoked a cigarette.

He placed his left hand on the steering wheel.
"What now?"

She folded the paper and placed it inside the
glove compartment. "They killed Rita."

He took a drag from his cigarette in dismay.
"What are we dealing with here?" Agitated smoke
escaped from his mouth. "This is Peggy Meachum
we're talking about. I'm *married* to this woman."

"Don't do that to yourself."

"Who am I, not to have known who *she* is?"

"You can't feel bad about that," she whispered.

"They want to kill us." He stared at the smoke
rising from his cigarette. "They have killed."

"Let's run away."

"We can't."

She looked out the window and saw the red flag in the parking meter pop up. "We're out of time."

He turned to her. "John Landruth."

"Who's that?"

"He's Tidewater Pub's marketing director, remember? I've told you about him."

"What about him?"

He placed the cigarette in the corner of his mouth and started the car. "He lives in Virginia Beach."

She didn't press him.

He maneuvered the vehicle out of the parking spot and merged into Granby Street's traffic.

Chapter 40

After traveling on Highway 264 toward Virginia Beach for a while, Susan decided to press Tony about John Landruth.

"Okay. Okay." He pulled the cigarette from his mouth. "He lives in a bungalow in Chick's Beach. He's an outgoing beach-buggy kind of guy with expensive taste. He likes to drive hard and party long."

"I've got the 'who' and the 'where,'" she said. "Now give me the 'what' and 'why.'"

"He was pretty chummy with Douglas and Rita—and Joe."

"So what? He's friendly. He's outgoing. That's how marketing guys are."

"There was more to John than that." He took a short drag from his cigarette. "He was the kind of guy who always had an angle, who always had a guarded grin. Yeah. I remember John now—and Joe."

"What about them?"

"They were closer than they led on to be." He nodded. "Yeah. Their office conversations were . . . were often whispered. That's it. They shared secrets."

"So you think Landruth might know something because they whispered?" she countered skeptically.

"Give me a break, Susan. I've got a hunch."

"And it's a thin one."

"John could know something. Besides, you said that there might be others in the company who are involved."

"And you said that you were not that important."

"You also said my books were worth a lot of money. John is all about the money." He took a final drag from his cigarette and crushed it out. "He sees the world in terms of earning a commission."

"There's nothing wrong with that."

It started raining.

"John worked in marketing, and I worked in public relations. We got along well near the coffee pot. We even shared the last doughnut a time or two."

Susan frowned.

"What's wrong?" Tony turned on the windshield wipers.

"The newspaper and Rita. Craig with his car. And—I've got a bad feeling."

"Don't start that, Susan."

"Let's go to the police."

"I can't. Something about myself is still missing."

"They've tried to kill us. The police would help."

"No police."

"But why?"

"It's against the law to kill yourself."

"You're here."

"I'm a fraud. I could go to jail for that."

"Not in today's legal system."

"There's been a murder. Maybe two murders associated with my whole Tony Wilson scheme. It's gotten way out of control. No police!" he shouted. "I'm an all-or-nothing kind of guy!"

"What the hell does *that* mean?"

"I'm about making it at all cost. I'm about getting even. I'm about getting revenge."

"Then you're just like Peggy!"

He gasped.

"I'm sorry."

"You're right." He turned on the headlights. "I'm thinking like Tony Wilson."

They fell silent as he drove.

"I think I understand now," she whispered. "You have to become Larry Meachum again, before—"

"—Tony destroys me. I have to finish this in *my* way—whatever that way is."

The rainstorm intensified. The wipers sliced furiously across the windshield.

He drove into the parking lot of a strip mall, parked the car, and turned off the engine.

"You didn't have to get angry at me," she said.

"I was angry about my *life*."

"I'm *in* your life."

"I'm sorry. But I'm worried that I might lose this battle."

"Then let's run away. At least we'll have each other."

He leaned toward her and caressed her face. "You're sweet."

She chuckled. "Nobody has ever accused me of that."

He kissed her on the cheek. "Stand accused." He released her and leaned against the driver-side door. "But no matter what happens, I hope I can get some of my money back."

"That's Tony Wilson talking again."

He grabbed the steering wheel with his left hand. "I've got to get my mind right before . . . before—"

"—you lose yourself completely."

"I want justice."

"That's Larry Meachum talking."

"I won't sacrifice you."

"Is that a Larry Meachum promise?"

He nodded. "But Peggy and Craig are not going to live happily ever after."

She did not try to soften his bitterness.

"My head still doesn't feel right."

"I'm here," she whispered tenderly.

"I might *never* feel right."

"I'll be right here."

He started the car and drove out of the parking lot. The rain was no longer threatening.

Chapter 41

After driving into Chick's Beach, Tony kept tapping the brakes with uncertainty until he decided to step on the brake at a street corner.

"Is this his place?" Susan asked.

"No."

"What's wrong?"

"It's been a while since I've been here."

"Take your time."

"My memory—it doesn't work as well since the accident."

"You're doing fine, honey."

He made a right turn, then slowed to a stop near a street curb. "Damn."

"What's wrong?"

"Look over there. That's Lois, leaving John's house."

"She's frightened."

Lois got into her car, started it, and drove away.

"Let's find out what's going on." Tony parked the car in the driveway. "Come on."

They stepped out of the car and approached the bungalow.

"I don't like this," Susan whispered.

He pressed the doorbell, then knocked on the door. No answer.

When he turned the doorknob, he discovered it was unlocked. He pushed open the door and stepped inside.

"Be careful." She followed him.

The living room was dark. Black curtains blocked out the sun. There was a sofa, a television, and four bare walls. The carpet was stained and threadbare.

"What do you think?" she whispered.

"I don't know." He crossed the living room and stepped into the kitchen. "Susan!"

"What?" She entered the kitchen.

John Landruth was hanging by his neck from a yellow nylon rope attached to an overhead pot-and-pan rack.

She cupped her mouth with both hands. "Landruth?"

"Yeah. No wonder Lois was frightened."

Chapter 42

They drove to Lois's house in Chesapeake. When they arrived, they discovered that her front door was ajar.

"That's odd," she whispered.

They approached the house.

He pushed open the door. "Lois?"

"Be careful."

They stepped inside.

Lois was sitting on a sofa. She was as pale as a white marble statue. Her bird-like figure appeared fragile underneath her pastel-green dress. Her red hair was disheveled. She had a Kleenex in her hand.

He approached her. "Are you alright?"

The living room was clean and orderly. There were porcelain vases on the fireplace mantel and oil paintings on the walls, and Ethan Allen furniture carefully arranged upon a white carpet.

She tried to repair her short hair. Tears stained her marble complexion. "I loved John."

"What happened?"

She didn't answer.

"Did you kill Joe?" he asked.

"Our marriage was a mess."

"Did you love him?"

"He was unfaithful."

"What happened to John?"

She sobbed. "I couldn't take him down." She pressed the Kleenex against her nose.

He waited.

She discarded the Kleenex and replaced it with a handkerchief. She blew her nose. "I loved him."

"What happened?"

"I need a cigarette."

He reached into his shirt pocket and pulled out a pack of cigarettes. He shook out a cigarette and offered it to her.

She pulled it out of the pack and waited for a light.

He shook out another cigarette for himself, then reached into his right trouser pocket and pulled out a cigarette lighter. "Suicide? Or murder?" He flipped open the lighter and struck the flint.

She leaned forward and stuck the tip of her cigarette into the flame, then leaned back on the sofa as she took a deep drag. Tony lit his cigarette. "Did John commit suicide?"

She exhaled. "It was murder."

"Who did it?"

"Craig Chadwick." She took another drag.

He glanced at Susan. She shook her head.

"I finally had enough of him," Lois said, "when he started seeing Peggy."

The crooked corners of Tony's mouth betrayed his bitterness. "I know Chadwick was seeing Peggy."

She wiped her nose with the handkerchief. "I was talking about Joe, not Chadwick."

"Oh." He took a hard drag from his cigarette. "Yeah. There was a time when I thought Joe was my friend."

"Joe was *nobody's* friend." She set aside her handkerchief.

"So, you started seeing John."

Lois flicked ash from her cigarette into an ashtray. "John was a good man. That's something Joe never was." She reached into her purse and pulled out a revolver.

"Hey! I'm on your side," said Tony.

"No, you're not. I did not kill Joe. Or Douglas."

Tony was startled. "Douglas killed?" He peered at Susan to convey alarm.

She stepped toward Lois. "That's my man you're pointing a gun at."

Lois took a calm drag from her cigarette.

"What do you know about Douglas?" Susan whispered.

"He was a nothing."

"How did you find out about his death?"

"Through John," said Lois.

"And?"

"What? You saw what happened to him. That knowledge cost John his life."

"And Douglas," Susan pondered, "may have been Rita Feldman's lover."

Lois studied the line of smoke rising from her lit cigarette. "Now that's something I did not consider." She brought the cigarette close to her mouth. "So?"

Susan stepped closer to her. "Who knew about Tony Wilson at Tidewater Publishing?"

"I don't know," Lois shrugged. "I didn't know anything about Tony Wilson. Joe—and John—kept me in the dark about that."

"You've got to help us," said Susan.

"Why should I?"

"Because Craig Chadwick killed your John."

Lois sneered. "Don't manipulate me."

"I'm not. I'm afraid."

Lois nodded. "Alright. I understand that." She crushed out her cigarette. "I thought Craig Chadwick was a friend of John's."

"Then you know Craig well," Susan added.

"Obviously not." She placed the revolver on her lap. "They worked closely on Larry Meachum's royalty account." She stole a glance at Tony. "Like I said, I didn't know anything about you being Tony Wilson. You were supposed to be dead."

"Larry Meachum was dead. Now look at him."

"Go on," said Susan. "What else did they do together?"

"I don't know. Craig worked with John who, apparently, worked with Rita who—"

"Worked with Douglas who worked with Joe who . . ." Tony crushed out his cigarette.

"Who worked with Peggy," Lois said, finishing his sentence. "According to John, Larry's royalties were going directly into their account."

"Wait a minute," Susan interjected. "Their account?"

"Yes," Lois said, "*their* account."

"You do mean Larry's and Peggy's account," Susan verified.

"Of course. Was there another?"

"What are you getting at, Susan?" Tony asked.

"Your account."

"What about it?"

"You might still have access to it."

"But Meachum is dead," he said.

"But it's possible that she never took your name off the joint account."

"Meaning what?"

"That the royalties were probably kept in Larry Meachum's name for continuity. You know, because she was your wife and, well, she had to keep your name on the bank account in order to keep control of the money. And since all the players at Tidewater Publishing were on her side, why would she change anything? Why would she take a chance of losing control of the income?"

"You might have something there, Susan. But I think the Commonwealth of Virginia requires that all financial accounts have to be settled with a death certificate within a year."

"Are you sure about that?" Susan challenged.

"I'm pretty sure," he said.

"You're wrong about that," said Lois.

"I am?"

"In Virginia," she continued, "joint bank accounts are always presumed to belong to the surviving party—your Peggy."

"Are you sure?"

"I've been the wife of a businessman throughout all the ups and the downs," Lois said. "Believe me. I know. As a surviving owner, Peggy can always withdraw and deposit money from the account—she has always had access to it. On the other hand, providing the bank with a death certificate would clear the deceased from the account. Then where would the royalties go?"

"That's lost control," said Susan.

"You're right," Tony added. "A death certificate has not been issued on Larry Meachum."

"How come?" Lois asked.

"Because Meachum's supposed suicide is still an open case," he said. "They never found the body."

"Well," said Lois, "there you are."

"Yeah. Here I am," said Tony.

"And there it is," Susan said. "Peggy hasn't taken you off the account because it's safer to keep you where you are."

"That's probably true. But I still don't have any identification, remember? No checkbook, no account number—nothing. How could I access it?"

"Okay. Fine." She turned to Lois. "Then let's get back to Peggy?"

"What *about* her?"

"There was no need to continue working with Joe."

"That's right," said Lois. "He was no longer useful." Grudging tears rolled down her cheeks. "Joe meant nothing to her. The poor slob." She addressed Tony. "Joe was a means to an end." She placed the revolver on the sofa. "Like you."

"And you saw this," Susan declared.

Lois wiped away her tears with her handkerchief. "I didn't know what I was seeing. Mister Tony Wilson here should be able to understand that."

Tony nodded as she took a drag from her cigarette.

Susan was careful to ask, "Why do you think Craig killed John?"

"When I saw John hanging from that rope, I remembered things," Lois said sadly. "It's odd what things comes to mind when confronted with something horrible."

"What *things?*" Susan whispered.

"When John found out about Douglas's death, he was really upset. Really afraid."

"Of *what?*"

"Of *Craig*—I think. But he wouldn't admit it. He denied he was afraid."

"Why?"

"I don't know." She sighed. "He wasn't good at concealing his emotions."

"Go on."

"Men. You know how they are. They always have to have their secrets. Even though they're bad at concealing them."

"And?"

"John didn't want to have anything more to do with Craig. He wanted out. He knew his life was in danger."

"I see."

"John was a kind man," Lois continued. "Not a great man. Not a sophisticated man. Not a smart man." Lois crushed out her cigarette without taking a final drag. "When John read about Rita Feldman's death in the newspaper—well, that was too much for him. He couldn't keep his mouth shut. He had to confront Chadwick about her. He had to . . . ."

She stared at the fragile wisp of smoke rising from the ash.

"Go on," said Susan.

Lois bowed her head. "One of them killed her," said Lois. "But Chadwick killed my man. I know this in my heart."

Chapter 43

Tony took a firm hold of the steering wheel with his left hand after he started the car. "Don't worry." He shifted the automatic transmission into reverse. "I'm not going to kill Craig."

"I'm glad we have an alliance with Lois."

"Yeah. She's tougher than her tears."

"What are you doing with her gun?" Susan asked.

"I couldn't let her keep it."

"Don't lie to me."

"I might have to use it."

"Why don't you use your head instead?"

He took his right foot off the brake. "Very funny." He backed out of the driveway into the street.

"Be smarter than Peggy for once."

He braked hard. "Okay. I deserved that." He shifted into drive, then stepped on the gas pedal. "Who killed Rita Feldman?"

"If it's Craig . . ."

"Yeah." He made a right turn at the first street corner. "And if it isn't . . ."

They reached the edge of the subdivision and stopped at the red light.

"Where are we going?" Susan asked.

He made a left turn when the traffic light turned green. "To Seashore State Park."

"Where's that?"

"In Virginia Beach. It's not far from Chick's Beach. Do you mind camping out tonight?"

"Not at all. But why?"

"I don't want to be closed in," he said. "I'd like to see the stars in the sky and listen to the ocean surf."

"I understand that."

"I want to sleep on the beach."

"That's fine with me."

He steered the car onto the entrance ramp of Interstate 64.

Chapter 44

The night sky was clear on the beach. The sound of the surf did not disappoint.

They had two large blankets spread out on the sand: one underneath them, the other on top. Slumber, however, was difficult for Susan because of Tony's troubled sleep and disturbing dreams where darkness met light and where reality met delusion, which pushed his identity against the four walls of existence that were closing in on Tony Wilson and Larry Meachum:

They stood together on the rim of a high plateau facing an infinite space.

They received all the visible spectrum of colors from the vast sky.

Everything suddenly became a wash of white light.

Tony felt the hard sand beneath him and Susan's loving presence beside him.

He opened his eyes. His mouth was so dry he couldn't speak.

"Go back to sleep," Susan whispered.

The freshness of a cool wind felt good.

He smiled. He closed his eyes. His mind turned white with light:

The sky pressed down upon the plateau where he stood facing himself.

"I want my life!" Larry demanded.

"I'm trying to help you!" Tony countered.

Red, blue, yellow, and each remaining color
in the visible spectrum of light disappeared
until darkness descended upon them.

Tony felt a tender hand touch his forehead.

He drifted. He struggled for control of himself:

"We can't be separate."

"I am the past."

"You are the future."

"We are one."

He sat up. "Hard battle."

She touched him as she whispered, "You were delirious."

His teeth chattered. "Why am I cold?"

She draped the top blanket over his shoulders. "You were lost in a troubled dream."

"I'm thirsty."

She searched for and found an unopened plastic bottle of spring water. "You had me worried." She twisted off the plastic cap and gave him the bottle.

He drank deeply.

She supported his back with the palm of her right hand and whispered, "Who won the battle?"

"I did."

Chapter 45

Moonlight bathed the evening shore.

Susan stirred from her slumber when Tony awoke, stood up, then approached the shoreline. She sat up on the blanket.

He faced the ocean for a long time, then approached the edge of their blanket. "Are you alright?"

"Are you?"

He rubbed his eyes with the back of his hands. "Something finally came to me."

"What?"

"I wanted to die when I had that head-on collision."

"Don't believe that."

"The other guy who was driving in my lane was drunk."

"There. You see?"

"But I think I could have swerved away."

"You're inventing this," she said. "You don't remember. You never will."

"But I could have—"

"No. I know you. It was an accident."

He sat beside her. "Okay. Okay."

She placed her right arm across his shoulders and hugged him.

"Joe and Peggy were in on it together from the beginning," he said.

"I know that."

"They were lovers."

"That's right. And?"

"My memory about what happened before the accident became clearer tonight."

"Tell me about it."

"I was working late at the office."

"At Tidewater Publishing?"

"Yes. I thought I was the only one left in the building that night. I decided to go to Joe's office to get the spare key to the building so I could lock up. But when I stepped into the hallway, I heard the edge of a strained conversation coming from his office."

"Go on."

"Joe was on the telephone, talking to Peggy about me. They were secret lovers who were planning my death. That's what happened. And they were laughing at me."

"That's terrible," she whispered.

"They were laughing."

"Don't be afraid of the truth."

He scoffed. "The truth." He reached into his shirt pocket—it was empty. "No cigarettes." He sighed. "I beat the hell out of Joe. I wanted to kill him—and her. But childish anger got the best of me and kept me from avoiding my accident."

"You don't know that."

"Maybe. But I do know that I'm weak in Peggy's eyes."

"Then use that." She grabbed the front of his shirt. "Use it against her, damn it." She released his shirt.

"Use it." He approached the shoreline, stepped ankle deep into the surf, sat down in the water, then planted his hands in the wet sand behind him to support himself.

She joined him, then sat down.

The surf washed over their legs.

"I was wrong yesterday," he muttered.

"About what?"

"About the joint bank account."

"Meachum is dead, remember? And he has no identification and—"

"I know," he said.

"So. Nothing. Remember? Nothing."

"That's still true."

"So?"

He leaned forward, washed the sand off his hands, then turned to her. "So, tomorrow I'll try to withdraw money from Peggy's bank account."

"That might be dangerous."

"It *will* be." He leaned toward her. "I want you to wait outside for me—with the car running."

"Because you won't succeed?"

"That's right. Without identification, I can't gain access to the account. But when I insist on it, the teller might become suspicious and call for the bank manager. That's when I'll leave. And that's when they might call the police. Even if they don't, they will certainly alert Peggy about my attempted breach on the account."

"Okay. But I don't understand."

"You don't have to."

"Okay."

"Do you love me?"

She leaned toward him. "Of course I do."

"Okay."

Book V

Craig Chadwick

Chapter 46

Craig had to take time off from work. He rarely took vacations at TeliCom because he didn't trust his coworkers. He didn't trust Peggy either. She was all about the money—and control.

Lola, his office assistant, startled him. "Mister Chadwick, are you alright?"

He glanced at her. "I'm sorry, Lola. I was thinking about the NAVSEA briefing. Be sure Harry gets all my telephone calls."

"Yes, sir."

He picked up a disc and gave it to her. "And give that to him. It's the marketing data concerning acquisitions & procurement. Instruct Harry on how we do our briefings."

"Yes, sir." She hesitated. "Is everything alright, Mister Chadwick?"

"Alright?" Her genuine concern caught him off-guard.

"Is there an illness in the family?"

"No, no, nothing like that." Craig leaned back in his chair and studied his loyal assistant. How could he tell her that he needed time off from work in order to commit another murder? "It's been a long time since I've taken a vacation. I'm way overdue."

"Do you think this is the right time for you to go? The NAVSEA account is heating up again and—"

"It's *never* a good time, Lola. You know that."

She nodded. "I will do my best for you while you're gone."

"I know you will."

She approached his office door.

"Please call me if anything urgent arises," he added.

"Of course." She stepped into the communal clerical room and went to her desk.

Craig leaned back in his office chair.

He remembered killing Joe. It seemed like he killed him yesterday. And that yesterday felt like today. *Now.*

Craig closed his eyes and remembered taking the day off from TeliCom.

He had driven to Norfolk and—

—and after he arrived, he got something to eat at a diner, then waited until late afternoon before calling Joe at the publishing house from an outside public telephone that was mounted to the sidewall of a convenience store where he had bought a pack of cigarettes.

Craig called Joe, but there was no answer. When he started to call again, he remembered that, according to Peggy, Joe was always in the warehouse at the end of each day.

"Damn," he muttered. He wasn't thinking clearly. "What's wrong with me?"

He drove to Tidewater Publishing's warehouse and, except for Joe's car, the parking lot was empty.

He stepped out of his black BMW and carefully shut the vehicle's door. Then he cautiously opened the side door of the little warehouse and entered quietly.

The fluorescent lamps above him flickered and blinked their need to be replaced. The cast of shadows did not remain in one place.

The warehouse was laid out in a confused mess of overcrowded stock, which burdened its maze of top-heavy wooden tiers.

What a cheesy operation, he thought.

He heard rummaging. He recognized the distinctive slap of a dropped book upon a floor and the dull thud of one being tossed carelessly into a box—that had to be Joe.

Instead of announcing himself, Craig approached what appeared to be a work table that was near a secured garage door that lead to a makeshift loading dock when it was open—he discovered a steel door-prop. He picked it up and assessed its deadly weight by gently thumping it against the palm of his left hand.

He estimated Joe's location by the sound of his continuous rummaging, then cautiously approached that sound via a parallel aisle until he saw Joe through a space between two book pallets that were stored on the second shelf of the tier between them.

Joe was preoccupied with his world of books, Craig thought.

He tiptoed to the end of his aisle, crept around both corners, then brazenly approached Joe from behind and struck him on the shoulder near the neck with the steel door-prop. Joe's shock into unconsciousness caused him to collapse onto the cement floor.

Not a word was said. No eye contact was made.

Easy-peasy, Craig thought. *Clean and bloodless and easy as pie.*

The tall and unsteady wooden tier beside Joe appeared to be a snap to topple over. However, Craig was surprised to discover how much muscle was required to accomplish this task.

Undeterred, Craig searched for and found a sixteen-foot aluminum stepladder. He carried it to the parallel aisle that he used to make his initial search for Joe, then maneuvered down the aisle until he found him again.

Craig opened the stepladder and parked it close to the flimsy tier so he could get high enough to rock and aggravate the overloaded structure until it reached the critical point of collapse. He held onto the top of the sixteen-foot stepladder, watched his accomplice-in-murder smash against another wooden tier on the other side of the aisle, then crash on top of Joe. What Craig discovered, after the wincing sound of splintering wood and breaking pallets came to an end, was the appearance of an official accident scene in the making. It was beautiful.

He stepped off the ladder, closed it, and put it back where he had found it.

He stopped for a moment, and considered what needed to be done to set a good fire before he left the scene.

He scanned the interior of the warehouse and discovered that Joe had neglected to have a fire alarm system installed.

On the cheap, he thought. *Great. Somehow Joe managed to escape the fire department's scrutiny, which will make this fire more probable. Nice. Tidewater Publishing was a shoestring operation, and this silly little warehouse reflected that.*

He chuckled. "Cheesy. Cheesy."

There was plenty of packing material, boxes, and papers; and yes, this place was a hazard just waiting for a fire to occur. However, he knew that the use of any flammable liquid would catch the attention of an arson investigator.

No liquids. Go natural. This had to appear to be an accident—a fire of unknown origin.

Craig approached the littered work table after retrieving the steel door-prop. When he tossed it onto the table, he noticed that someone had left behind their pack of cigarettes and lighter. A fiendish smile spread across his face.

"A smoldering cigarette could contribute to a fire of unknown origin," he whispered.

He reached for the pack of cigarettes and lighter, lit a cigarette, then tossed the pack and lighter back onto the table.

He glanced at the body underneath the rubble and realized that Joe had been personally staging a book shipment for whatever reason. Joe was a small-minded micro manager, and that kind of guy always irritated him.

Ah. He noticed that, in addition to the two ashtrays on the work table, there was an ashtray near the staging area where Joe had been working. *More possible evidence toward a cause that might survive the fire. Ashtrays.* He grimaced, after taking a drag. *And cigarettes*, he thought to himself. He was determined to consider every detail, even though the fire would probably consume the cigarette.

He approached and assessed the debris on top of Joe. The broken tiers were made of cheap and porous pine that would burn readily. The broken pallets of books, on the other hand, not so readily.

No matter, he thought. *There's plenty of time for the fire to catch. Let's see: no windows, closed doors, contained space. Nice.*

The destructive fire would spread throughout the warehouse before someone noticed or smelled any smoke escaping from a vent, and before anyone finally called the fire department—the arrival of the first-in engine would be met with a lot of fire.

By the time the body was discovered, there shouldn't be any evidence that would lead an arson investigator to consider Joe's death a murder.

Craig was pleased with himself.

He took a deep drag from the cigarette to intensify its smolder, then tossed the half-smoked cigarette onto a wad of packing material.

"There." He struck the flint of his cigarette lighter. "That smoldering cigarette will need help."

Yes. Clean and bloodless.

He studied the small flame. It was radiant enough to help brighten his outlook. Later, that flame would not be enough to thwart his growing darkness associated with Douglas's murder. Even though that execution also took place from behind, it was neither clean nor bloodless. And because Craig's intent to shoot him was discovered moments before the trigger was pulled, Douglas had time to utter a short cry of terror. This made Craig flinch and panic into a second shot. A clumsy act, which forced him to study the result.

He saw two irregular dark splatters, but only one black bullet hole was accompanied by two trickles of red blood that seemed to have coagulated mid stream. That seductive image of what he believed to be the first shot, combined with Douglas's thin-pitched cry, haunted him.

The sound of a ringing telephone in the clerical room startled him back into the present. He sat up, leaned toward his desk, and shook himself free from his dark thoughts.

He opened his eyes and stared at the large computer screen that dominated the left side of his desk. The glow of the screen's text upon the dark background taunted him with the unfinished work that he had to complete before he could leave the office that afternoon.

He was unable to keep his mind on his work.

Craig used to like the finer things in life: food and drink, sports and gambling, fast cars and fine women. But after getting involved with Peggy, he ate badly and drank too much, he lost interest in sports and lost money playing poker, he abused his car and resented all women.

He stood up and went to the restroom.

It was a single-use public restroom: one toilet, one sink, locked door.

Craig approached the sink and examined himself in the mirror above it. He wasn't pleased by what he saw. Deceit and homicide had produced dark half-circle bags under his eyes. He pressed his right cheek with his left forefinger in an effort to flatten a bag; it became longer instead. "Damn." He also needed a haircut.

Leaving Pamela and his daughter, Jenny, had been easy compared to getting involved with Peggy Meachum—an emotional vampire. Her needs were endless, her desires were insatiable. Nothing was ever enough, even murder—a deed that had stripped him of his spirit and had left him feeling exhausted. He was troubled by what had been done, and by what *had* to be done. She was not. This disturbed him; and yet, he couldn't break free from this strange attraction he had for her, this strange hold she had on his life.

He wanted to punch that image in the mirror, but bowed his head and leaned against the sink instead.

"Get a grip. There's no getting away from yourself, Chadwick. You have to finish this thing soon and get it behind you."

Craig washed his face with warm water, then yanked several brown paper towels from the dispenser and dried his face and hands.

Someone knocked on the door.

"I'll be out in a minute."

Nobody was standing outside when he unlocked the door.

He went back to his office and sat behind his desk. As he reached for a folder, the telephone rang. He picked up the receiver.

"Hello?"

"Craig?"

"Peggy."

"We're in trouble."

"Talk."

"Not on the telephone."

"Tell me something."

"It's . . . it's about the money."

"What about it?"

"I'll see you after work."

"Peggy."

She hung up the telephone.

"Peggy!" He snarled at the telephone receiver, then slammed it onto the cradle. "Damn that woman!" He rose from his chair and peered into the clerical room.

His office assistant pretended that she did not hear his outburst. The others in the clerical room pretended as well. It was a bad performance.

Craig maneuvered around his desk, approached the wall to the left of the door to obstruct their view of him, then pressed his back against the wall and wondered what it would have been like if everything had remained as it was before—when the two of them were lovers without a future.

Chapter 47

Chadwick left work early.

When he got home, he loosened his tie, poured himself a Scotch, and drank it. Then he took off his jacket and tossed it onto a chair.

He poured himself another Scotch, sat on the sofa, and tried to relax.

When Peggy arrived, she sighed to convey her discontent.

Craig did not look at her. "What about the money?"

"The money's gone," she answered.

"Stop playing around."

"I'm not playing."

"How?" he demanded.

She did not reply as she approached him.

Craig placed his empty glass on the side table, rose from the sofa, and grabbed her by the throat. "Don't swindle me."

He threw her on the sofa and enjoyed her gasps. "The money."

"You brute." She massaged her throat. "It's gone."

Craig's hands shook. "Tell me how."

"I don't know."

He poured himself another drink. "One more time. The money."

She stood up. "Larry Meachum."

He tossed down the Scotch. "I thought he was out of the picture. I thought you had him under control."

"I thought I did. But somehow Larry was able to enter my bank account and withdraw everything."

"How is that possible?"

"I don't know."

"Don't tell me you didn't drop his name from the joint account."

She bit her lower lip. "I didn't."

"Damn! How stupid!"

"I didn't think he would be—"

"Smarter than you?" He threw his glass across the room.

She approached him. "Lois."

He grimaced. "Lois what?"

"Larry called and told me to meet him at Lois's house tomorrow."

He raised his arms to convey his exasperation. "How the hell did he manage to get Lois involved into this . . . this *whatever* he's doing?"

"I don't know."

"He called you!" Craig cackled. "God help me!" He poured another drink and offered her the glass. "Here. You're no smarter than I am."

She accepted Scotch. "I'm sorry."

His sigh conveyed disgust. "Isn't there any way of getting it back?"

"The money has been transferred to a new account." She shook her head. "That's all the bank manager was able to tell me."

"Is that legal?"

She shrugged. "They did it."

"But how?"

"I don't know."

"By whose authority?"

"I don't know."

Craig grabbed his sports jacket, approached the front door, and opened it.

"Where are you going?"

"*We* are going to Chesapeake. We're not waiting until tomorrow."

She followed him outside.

He approached his vehicle, opened the driver-side door, and sat behind the steering wheel. "Do you remember how to get to Lois's place?"

"Of course." She opened the passenger-side door of his BMW, sat down, and shut the door. "What are we going to do when we get there?"

He started the car and shifted the transmission into drive. "I don't know."

Chapter 48

Craig pressed the lit end of his cigarette butt against the tip of the fresh cigarette hanging from his mouth, puffed on it until there was smoke, then cracked open the window and tossed out the spent cigarette. He enjoyed watching the sparks explode from the butt bouncing against the pavement through the rearview mirror.

"What are you doing?" Peggy demanded.

"I'm smoking another cigarette."

Peggy was exasperated, as she crushed out her cigarette into the dashboard's ashtray. "It's late. We've been cruising around all evening. I thought we were going to Chesapeake."

"We are."

"What are you waiting for?"

"Darkness."

"It *is* dark."

"*More* darkness. I want them to feel safe. They're not expecting us tonight."

"You evil bastard."

He took a hard drag from his unfinished cigarette, cracked open the window, and threw it out. "Okay. I'm ready."

"Make a right turn on the next intersection," she said.

Once they arrived, Craig intentionally drove past Lois's house. The exterior light above the front door and the interior lights of the house were on. He made a left turn at the first corner, then came to a stop halfway down the street.

"What are we doing?" Peggy asked.

"This is where I get out."

Peggy reached into her purse and pulled out a revolver. "You'll need this."

"Where did you get that?"

"I had another."

He took the revolver. "Is it registered?"

"No."

He made sure the revolver was loaded, then inserted it inside of his left jacket pocket. "I want you to take the car and drive around until I turn off the exterior light above the door. That's your signal to come to the house." He opened the door and stepped out of the car. "Take the wheel."

She opened the passenger-side door, stepped out, and walked around the rear of the BMW to his side.

"Leave the key in the ignition after you park." He shut the door after she sat behind the steering wheel.

She rolled down the window. "Be careful, Craig."

"Now she tells me."

"I mean it."

"Let's get this over with."

"I love you."

"Yeah, yeah—go on."

She rolled up the window and drove away, as he walked toward the house.

Once there, he maneuvered into the backyard and approached the house's screened-in porch—it was unlocked.

Craig stepped onto the dark porch, approached a back door that lead into a kitchen, and discovered that it was unlocked. "Stupid."

He pulled out the revolver, after stepping into the kitchen, and decided to be reckless—he barged into the living room and surprised Lois. "Where are they?"

"Craig!" She rose from the sofa.

"Where's Tony and Susan?"

"I don't know."

He slapped her face, then pushed her onto the sofa. "Stay there." He made a quick search throughout the house, then went to the front door and turned off the exterior light. "Alright, Lois, I'll ask you again. Where are they?"

"They . . . they've gone to the office."

"What office?"

"Tidewater Publishing."

A tap on the front door drew his attention away from her. He crossed the living room, peered through a security hole to see if it was Peggy, then opened the door.

She stepped inside and saw Lois. "Where are the others?"

He shut the door. "She says they're at Tidewater Publishing."

She approached Lois. "Call them."

"They could be anywhere in the building."

"Call them."

"They probably won't answer."

"I'm sure you've arranged a code." Peggy grimaced. "Craig? Do something with her."

He stepped toward Lois and threatened to strike her with the back of his left hand.

"Two rings and a hang-up. Then one ring and a hang-up."

He smirked after lowering his hand.

"Call them," Peggy demanded.

"And tell them what?"

"Tell them that I called you and that I plan to be here by eleven o'clock. Tell them to get here before I do. Tell them whatever you have to tell them to get them here."

Lois went to the telephone, picked up the receiver, and made the call.

Chapter 49

The doorbell rang.

"Answer it," Peggy whispered.

Lois rose from the sofa.

"I'll be in the kitchen, Craig."

The doorbell rang a second time."

"Answer it," Craig commanded, as he accompanied Lois. He pressed the revolver's muzzle against her side. "Don't be heroic." He placed himself on the hinged side of the door. "Open it."

Lois opened the door, and invited Tony and Susan inside.

"We came back as soon as we could," said Tony. "Bad traffic."

"That doesn't matter," said Lois. "I'm sorry. They forced me to call you."

As soon as Peggy stepped into the living room, Tony reached for his revolver.

Craig pushed the door closed. "Don't."

Tony hesitated.

"You're a dead man if you pull that gun." He kept his distance from Tony. "Take the gun from your belt and place it on the coffee table. Good. Step away from it." Craig approached the coffee table and picked it up. "Alright." He glanced at Susan. "You. Go to the sofa and sit down. You too, Lois. Go on!" He approached Peggy and gave her Tony's revolver.

She pointed the revolver at this strange person with familiar eyes. She was disturbed by the change in Larry's face. "I want my money."

"Ah. The money."

"She wants what?" Susan interjected.

"The money." Tony peered at her and emphasized, "*The money*."

Susan hesitated, then nodded. "Yes. The money."

Lois didn't understand what was going on, but she taunted Peggy anyway. "Look at her. She wants the money."

"Shut up!" Craig threatened to hit Lois, then glared at Tony. "The money."

Tony sneered at Peggy. "The dirty money."

"We want it," said Peggy. "And don't tell us it's in the bank."

"Where is it?" Craig demanded.

"It's not here," said Tony.

"Where is it!"

"I'll have to take you to it."

Peggy approached Craig. "If he's lying . . ." A mean expression spread across Peggy's hardened features. "Take my dead husband out for a drive and make sure he becomes the ghost that he's supposed to be. I'll take care of these two."

Craig leaned toward her. "Don't do anything to them until I get back."

"Why?" Peggy murmured.

"Because if he doesn't take me to the money, maybe one of *them* will. Can you handle them?"

"I'll shoot the first one that—"

"Easy, honey. Easy." He pointed his revolver at Tony. "Come on. Let's go."

Book VI

Tony Wilson

Chapter 50

The night was overcast. The neighborhood was dark.

Craig pressed the muzzle of his revolver against Tony's lower back, as he searched for where Peggy had parked his BMW. "Okay. Over there. To your left."

They approached the vehicle.

"Stand aside."

Tony remained calm and waited for Craig to make a mistake.

Craig opened the driver-side door. "Get in."

Tony sat behind the steering wheel. "How did you know?"

Craig shut the door, hustled to the other side, and opened the passenger-side door. He pointed the revolver at Tony. "Know *what*?"

"That I was the Larry Meachum you were trying to kill with this car."

Craig sat in the passenger seat. "I saw you leave Kirkpatrick's place that morning." He closed the door. "Start the car."

Tony was surprised to find the key in the ignition. "You didn't know for sure that—"

"I was sure enough to start that house fire. Drive. Take me to the money."

Tony started the car, shifted the car into drive, and stepped on the gas pedal. "You bastard." They were on Interstate 64 before he spoke again. "Peggy is no good."

"Neither am I."

"But you're also stupid."

"Shut up."

Tony drove. "Did Peggy give you a great performance about how the money was lost?"

"What are you talking about?"

"Did she press your buttons?"

"I'll press yours."

Tony drove. "I thought so."

"Shut up."

"Did she make you angry?"

"About what?"

"About the money, stupid."

"What about it?"

"*The money*." Tony drove. "Do you believe her story?"

"I'm going to hurt you."

"What did she tell you?"

"She said the money was gone. Withdrawn."

"Of course she did," he taunted. "And you believed her?"

Craig squirmed in his seat.

Tony laughed. "Come on. How is that possible? You know her."

"Shut up," said Craig with a rising anger. "I've killed three people and—"

"You mean, four," said Tony. "Don't forget Rita."

Craig laughed. "It was your *wife* that didn't forget Rita."

Tony stepped on the gas pedal in response.

"Slow down," said Craig.

Tony touched the brakes. "Peggy killed her?"

"That's right. With a hammer." Craig was pleased by Tony's shocked expression. "Don't worry. She'll be more humane with Susan and Lois when I get back with the money."

"You son-of-a-bitch."

"Stop talking."

Tony drove. "Let's see: A dead man without identification trying to withdraw cash from a Larry Meachum account—really?" he jibed. "That's ripe. That guy would have been challenged so fast that he would have left the bank before the teller had time to consult the manager." He felt the revolver's muzzle against his right side. "Easy there. Don't get nervous."

"Shut up."

"She's made a fool of you. And me."

"I said shut up, shut up!" Craig pulled the gun away in a fit of anger.

Mistake. Tony hit the brake pedal so hard that Craig hit his head on the dashboard. Then Tony let go of the wheel and grabbed Craig's left arm with his right hand and grabbed the revolver with his left.

They struggled. The vehicle swerved along the highway.

Gun shot.

The driver-side window shattered.

Gun shot.

When Tony smashed Craig's wrist against the steering wheel, the revolver fell to the floor.

The BMW skidded off the highway into the center median and spun around several times in the grass before it came to a stop.

After Craig's stunning blow to Tony's right temple, which knocked him against the car door, Craig retrieved the revolver. But Tony managed to grab Craig's wrist and divert the gun.

They struggled.

A gun shot.

Craig's arm relaxed.

Another gun shot.

Craig slumped against the passenger-door.

After catching his breath, Tony heard the distant bark of a dog and the distant sound of a siren.

He touched Craig and confirmed death, then opened the driver-side door and stepped out of the vehicle.

He could stand.

The siren grew closer.

"Damn." He walked to the edge of the grass median, crossed the southbound side of the highway, and hustled down the highway's shoulder toward a heavy growth of shrubbery. He was hidden from view by the time the police car arrived. The sirens of fire-and-rescue were closing in.

He climbed over a chain-linked fence and jumped into the backyard of a house.

He waited.

No barking dog.

He caught his breath.

No alarmed resident.

He walked along the side of the house and turned left when he reached a sidewalk. Then he walked through the subdivision until he reached a major thoroughfare and saw a convenience store across the street. He went into the store and discovered that it had a public restroom. He entered the restroom, locked himself inside one of two bathroom stalls, and sat on the toilet to rest.

A man entered the restroom and relieved himself at the urinal, which he did not flush, then left without washing his hands.

"I have to get back to that house," Tony whispered to himself. "I've got to save Susan and Lois."

He unlocked the door, stepped out of the stall, and approached the sink. He looked at himself in the mirror above the sink. "Not too bad."

He washed his hands and face. Everything hurt.

He left the bathroom and entered the main floor of the store.

Overhead fluorescent lights illuminated the store's aisles and the shelves that were stocked with cakes and candy and potato chips. He walked past a wall of refrigerators with glass doors that revealed their stock of beer and wine and soft drinks. He approached the end of a three-person line that led to the convenience store's checkout counter—two men and a woman were ahead of him. There were no conversations; only transactions could be heard at the counter that was serviced by an elderly East Indian man. When he reached the counter, he bought a pack of cigarettes.

He walked out of the convenience store and approached the left side of the structure.

No pay telephone.

He pulled off the cigarette pack's clear cellophane wrapper, tore out the pack's square silver top, and threw both wrappers into a trash can. He tapped the opened pack against the edge of his left hand and plucked a cigarette from the tight cluster that emerged from the square opening of the pack.

Tony placed the cigarette in the right corner of his mouth, lit it, then stepped onto the parking lot. A deep drag followed by a long exhale of gray smoke accompanied him as he crossed the parking lot. He avoided several vehicles: one departing and two entering.

He walked for a long time along the thoroughfare until he reached another convenience store. It had a row of three public telephones built into the store's cinder block side-wall. There were telephone books resting inside plastic cradles under each open-air booth.

He approached one of them and raised the hinged telephone book up to the booth's narrow counter underneath the change box. After noting the 1985 date printed on the tattered cover, he opened the book and searched for a taxi cab company that would drive him to Chesapeake.

He lifted the receiver off the hook and deposited a quarter into the pay telephone. He placed the receiver against his ear and waited to hear a clear tone before he dialed the number.

He sensed an uncertain future as the telephone rang.

Chapter 51

"Pull over into that parking lot up ahead," said Tony.

"Right." The cab driver drove into a strip mall's parking lot. All the stores were closed.

"Are you sure this is where—"

"Keep the change." Tony gave him a twenty-dollar bill.

"Thanks."

Tony stepped out of the taxi cab and watched the taxi drive away. Then he walked to the nearest street corner and turned right.

Lois's house was not far.

He smoked and walked and worried about Susan and Lois.

He reached Lois's backyard from the parallel street behind her house.

No dogs. No fence. No back light.

He entered the screened-in porch, approached the back door, and discovered it was unlocked.

After opening the door, he stepped into the dark kitchen, and exhaled with relief. Then crossed the kitchen, approached the entrance leading into the living room, and peered inside.

Peggy was sitting in a chair with her back to him. She had her revolver pointed at Susan and Lois. They were sitting on the sofa facing him.

Peggy caught the change in their expressions.

Tony rushed into the room and tackled Peggy before she could turn around.

Gun shot.

She dropped the revolver after he punched her in the stomach, then she rolled onto her side and brought her knees up to her abdomen.

He stood up. "It's over, Peggy." He picked up the revolver.

She struggled for breath. She managed to sit up. "Where's . . . where's Craig?"

Tony gestured to Susan and Lois to stay where they were. "You're plan didn't work, Peggy. He's dead."

"Damn him."

"Are you happy now?"

She stood up. "Kill me."

Her contempt frightened him. "Rita Feldman, John Landruth, Joe Gagliano, and Douglas Turner."

She shook her head. "You think you know something."

"I know nothing."

"How profound." Her sarcasm was deepened by the bitterness in her eyes.

"Call the police, Susan. It's time. It's time for Tony Wilson to tell the truth, *and* declare that he is Larry Meachum."

"I'll make that call," said Lois.

"The truth," Peggy muttered with contempt. "The truth."

Chapter 52

Larry and Susan stood outside the police station for a long time before she spoke. "I was surprised when you went along with Peggy about the money. She knew you didn't have it."

"That was the point of our going to the bank in the first place. The bank had to have told her about my attempt to breach her account. Remember?"

"I know that," she countered. "But at the time, I was frightened."

"You had every right to be."

"I wasn't thinking clearly."

"And I didn't know what I was doing or how it was going to work after I bought us some time. How is that for clear thinking?"

"You're scaring me, again."

"I'm sorry about that. But the truth is—you were right to be scared when I made that play against Peggy. I didn't know that the result of my going to the bank would present itself in this manner. I was improvising. I was trying to save our lives."

"And I almost blew it."

"But you didn't." He shook his head. "That Peggy—cold. She knew I didn't have the money—calculating. She gambled that I would lose my fight with Craig—vile. It was all or nothing for her—selfish." He sighed. "It still amazes me. She wanted Craig to kill me—then have him kill you and Lois."

"I don't know about that. She was pretty scary at the house after you and Craig left. Believe me, she was thinking about killing me and Lois even though Craig told her not to."

"I think that would have been too messy for her."

"Too messy for the girl with a hammer, you think?"

"Good point." He shuddered. "What do I know?" And with disgust, "She would have searched for a way to get rid of Craig as well. She had to."

"How dreadful."

"Stunning, really. But I made sure Craig understood Peggy's ultimate intent by taunting him about her during our drive."

"What a shock that must have been."

"It was—truly. My harassment about her betrayal made him so angry that it gave me the advantage I needed to overtake him in the car." He slipped his hands into his trouser pockets. "I didn't mean to kill him."

She trembled. "I know."

He pulled his hands out of the pockets, placed his right arm along the top of her shoulders, and gave her a gentle hug. "Thank you for having faith in me." He released her shoulders and faced her. "We've got a long way to go—legally."

"I know that." She shrugged. "What else have we got to do?"

"We almost lost everything."

"We're alive."

"Is that enough?"

"For me it is."

"Are you sure?"

"Shut up, Larry Meachum. I'm hungry."

The day was bright and beautiful; white clouds filled the blue sky.

The city was loud and congested; heavy traffic filled the tarred streets.

They walked on the sidewalk toward a small but real destination. And for them, that was enough.

About the Author

D. S. Lliteras is the author of fifteen books that have received national and international acclaim. His short stories have appeared in numerous national and international magazines, journals, and anthologies. He lives in Montgomery, Alabama with his wife and fellow author, Kathleen Touchstone.

Previous Books by D.S. Lliteras

Flames and Smoke Visible
"There is a hard-earned
wisdom in these true-life episodes."
—*Publishers Weekly*

Viet Man
"Forcefully written . . . has much to say
about life and death, and war and peace."
—*Booklist*

Syllables of Rain
"This slim novel will leave a lasting impression."
—*Library Journal*

Descent
"This is a brilliant little novel."
—*San Francisco Review of Books*

Rainbow Ridge Books publishes spiritual, metaphysical,
and self-help titles, and is distributed by Square
One Publishers in Garden City Park, New York.

To contact authors and editors, peruse our titles,
and see submission guidelines, please visit
our website at www.rainbowridgebooks.com.

For orders and catalogs, please
call toll-free: (877) 900-BOOK.